Authors Note: This is a work of fiction. Historical figures are characterized in ways consistent with known facts. Otherwise, the names, characters, and incidents are a product of the author's imagination.

Book Layout ©2013 BookDesignTemplates.com

Ordering Information: www.stancutlertauthor.com

LOW LIGHT/Stanley Cutler – 2nd edition
ISBN 978-0-9857343-1-2

LOW LIGHT

A Novel

by Stanley Cutler

Published by The Author

Philadelphia, Pennsylvania

PART ONE

Dangerous Offer

It started in April with the long distance, person-to-person call from my wife's cousin the gangster, Sam Brodsky. He wanted to offer me a job, he told me, one that would pay a lot, one that he chose not to discuss over the telephone. My first thought, when he came on the line, had been that he wanted to spread a little of his money around by having me take the pictures at his June wedding. I dropped a hint, which he ignored. Instead, he told me that his fiancée was a lovely girl named Anne whom everybody in the family would love. I told him that Ida, who is Sam's first cousin, and our two daughters were fine. Pretty soon we were done reminding each other that we were family, and Sam got down to business.

"Al, I have a job for you," he said. "You are the perfect guy for it. It's a special kind of photography. I don't even know for sure if it can be done."

I thought he was being secretive because he was worried about nosey neighbors on the party line or that the operator might be listening. It did not occur to me that he was worried about wiretaps by the Investigations Bureau of the United States Department of Justice. At that time, I was just an ordinary businessman who didn't even know there were such things as wiretaps. As I recall, I had never even heard of the Investigations Bureau.

"So why don't you come down to Philadelphia, and we'll talk about it," I said. "I'll show you my studio. You'll see, I have some terrific equipment, I can take just about any kind of picture."

"I've got a better idea," he said. "The picture has to be taken in Atlantic City. Why don't you meet me here? I'm staying at the new Ritz."

"Sam, it's barely even April. Who goes to Atlantic City at this time of year?"

"Al, I guarantee that it will be worth your while. We'll have dinner at the best restaurant in town. We'll go to a few night spots where, I guarantee, you'll have a great time. If you want to stay over, I'll get you a room at my hotel. Everything'll be on me. We'll have some fun... talk some business."

Ida and I had always suspected that Sam was into something that was on the shady side. We didn't know what kind of business it might have been, although we were aware of rumors that Sam worked for Arnold Rothstein, the New York gangster, the famous "Mr. Big" who was supposed to have fixed the 1919 World Series, and who'd been murdered in November of 1928 – front page news, even in Philadelphia.

After supper, as the girls were cleaning up the kitchen, I sat down with Ida in her sewing room and told her all about Sam's call. She was as curious as I. We speculated about the kind of photography Sam might have in mind. "Just be careful," she had said. "Don't agree to anything until we discuss it."

§

In summertime, because traffic backed up in the one-horse towns between Philadelphia and the resort, the ride to Atlantic City usually took three hours. On that gray April day, with little patches of snow still in the furrows in the fields, I made the drive in a little over two hours. Because I was early, I went onto The Boardwalk in front of the hotel to stretch my legs.

Seagulls were wheeling in the wind above the boarded-up cabanas; others stood on the rippled beach and watched the surf. I thought about the tricks I could use to capture the wintry feel of the place. I'd use a wide-angle lens. After developing the negative, I'd expose the paper in stages, using cutouts and stencils for the gulls and the cabanas. I'd make the gulls brighter against the sand and the sky, the cabanas, perhaps, darker. So, I ended up being a little late to see Sam because I was working on pictures in my head.

A doorman in a red coat touched the brim of his top hat and opened the door to the newest, fanciest hotel in town. The desk clerk, after he called Sam's room, told me to wait for someone to come and get me. A few minutes later, a short man with a waxed handlebar moustache,

3

wide shoulders and muscles that bulged against his suit, emerged from the elevator and spotted me waiting for him.

"Rubin? Follow me, please," he said with a Russian accent.

You needed to use two elevators to get up to Sam's place. An operator closed the brass lattice on the first elevator and took us to the eighth floor. We crossed the corridor to a smaller elevator that Mr. Moustache operated himself. The dial was all the way over, pointing to the gold "Penthouse" letters when the car stopped. The strongman gave a little bow and gestured for me to step out.

I realize, now, that the beautiful things I saw in Sam's penthouse got to me. The first thing I liked about the place was the view. I liked looking *down* at the wheeling gulls, at the unobstructed view of the sky, at how the low sun painted the towering clouds orange and pink, at the vast spread of the cold Atlantic. I liked the way the white rug, the first one I'd ever seen, made the room seem bright. There were real oil paintings on the walls, the kind you see in museums. The furniture was all smooth curves and hard edges, the latest style. A bronze statuette of a dancing woman graced the corner of a desk that was almost as big as my darkroom.

From behind the desk, Sam capped his fountain pen, closed the ledger book in front of him, and rose to greet me. I was struck, as I usually was after not seeing him for awhile, by his small stature, only an inch or two above five feet tall. His sleeves were rolled up to the elbow, his suit jacket draped over the back of his chair. As always, I was happy to see Sam, a man I regarded as a friend as well as a relative.

"Al," he said, smiling, "How's, Ida? How's business?"

"Good, good." I said. We'd never had a visit from Sam, so I told him all about my building in Southwest Philadelphia: '*Albert Photographic Studio*' in gilt-lettering on the storefront window; the darkroom in the back; our three-bedroom apartment upstairs. The property had a long backyard where Ida grew flowers and vegetables in the summer. The building was in a row of stores, a few doors down from a corner trolley stop, so there was a decent walk-in trade. When I told him how I'd been trying to hire somebody to help in the darkroom, I saw that he was losing interest. "Sam, I can't complain. And your business, Sam? How's by you?"

He shrugged. "Good, good." I was not surprised that he didn't elaborate. Then he got down to cases. "Al," he said, "What I wanted to ask you about was taking pictures outside your studio. Do you do that?"

"Sure, all the time. I have a couple of cameras I *schlep* around to weddings, to the high school for yearbook portraits, you know. I sometimes take them over to the park, down by the creek. I've even got pictures of birds." I mentioned my pigeon pictures, how I was proud of the way I'd captured the sheen of their ruffs. "But do you want that kind of stuff?"

5

"No. Nothing like that. I guess I wonder whether you can take pictures inside like it was outside. You know, without the flash powder and the sitting still and all."

"It depends," I said. "You mean taking candid pictures indoors?"

"Yes. Exactly. Taking candid pictures indoors."

I said, "I'd use bulbs instead of powder. That's how we're going to do it from now on. They've just come out with an attachment I can get for the side of my camera that's wired to the shutter and to a miniature dry cell battery. You press the shutter lever, and POOOF, you got just as good light as with the powder. At least that's what the Kodak people write in the advertisements. I was thinking of getting one anyway."

Sam seemed disappointed. "But people know you're taking their picture, right?"

"Hard not to."

He frowned and walked toward the window. He put his fingers into his back pockets and stared out at the horizon. "There's no way to take a picture without people knowing?" he asked.

I thought it over. "You could do it easy, if the people were outside and if it was daytime and they weren't walking or talking or anything."

He turned to me, frowning, and asked, "It can't be from the next room? Like through a little hole?"

"It could be inside," I replied. "But your subjects would have to be in a room with windows. Maybe like this one, with the sun coming right in and bouncing off a white rug and white walls. So, I'm saying, you *could* get a good picture, but it would have to be in the right room on the right day. And, yeah, you could set up your camera behind a wall."

Sam faced the wide French balcony doors. It was dusk; we watched a lamplighter on the Boardwalk far below lean his ladder against a post. The gas lamp flared, setting an aura of sea mist aglow.

"What's this about, Sam? Why don't you want people to know you're taking their picture?"

Sam thought for a moment, lips pursed, and came to a decision. "It's simple, Al. I need to get the goods on a man who's coming to this hotel on Decoration Day. He's in a very important job where he has to be Mr. Perfection. If I get a picture of him doing dirty stuff, I can solve many problems."

Sam turned from the window. "This guy we're talking about has been here in Atlantic City more than a few times, and he always comes with a pal. He may even be a *faygelleh*, this guy. There's a good chance he is, and if I have a picture of him naked with another man, that would be terrific. But maybe him and his pal get whores. I don't know. I do know that grownups don't come here for the saltwater taffy. A million men come to Atlantic City every year because they can do stuff here that they're afraid of getting caught doing back home. They want to believe that whatever happens in Atlantic City stays in Atlantic City."

Sam looked at me to see whether I was shocked. I kept a poker face. I knew right away, absolutely, that I didn't want anything to do with Sam's plan – I'm not a blackmailer. I should have said 'goodbye' right then. But I didn't. Partly, I didn't want Sam to think I was condemning him. Also, I wanted to act like a man of the world, a guy who looked on blackmail as an everyday sort of thing. Hah! But there was also the fact that I liked where I was. Sam's world, surrounded by the finer things in life, was more beautiful than mine. Being in that room, with its beautiful view and elegant objects, had an effect. I admit it, now.

"So who is he?" I asked.

"Did you ever hear of John Edgar Hoover?"

"Who's he? The President's brother?"

Sam sat down on the couch and lit a cigarette. "He's an official with the Department of Justice, in charge of the Investigations Bureau. He's not even related to the President. But he is a holier-than-thou, anti-Semitic son of a bitch. He's the guy who got Emma Goldman deported. He ran the Palmer Raids right after the War. Remember when they rounded up all those immigrants and said they were bomb throwers and union organizers and Anarchists and Communists? Hoover's the one who had the names of the people who got picked up. He has a file on anybody who ever went to a meeting or carried a picket sign. J. Edgar Hoover's the one who sent the marshals and had those people thrown in jail. Only a few of them had ever even given a speech, let alone thrown anything.

He personally saw to it that hundreds of them were deported, so he ruined all those families just by snapping his fingers. None of 'em ever got a trial.

"Now," said Sam, his voice rising, "Now, what with all the headlines about Tommy guns from Chicago and other towns, now the bastard has decided to come after us."

Us? Who's us?

I'd known Sam since his Bar Mitzvah; I just could not imagine him with a Tommy gun. I still can't.

I stared out into the dark. Seven gangsters had been Tommy-gunned in a Chicago garage on St. Valentine's Day, a gruesome massacre. The newspapers showed photos and ran editorials about how gangsters were taking over our streets, and how the government should be doing more about it. The whole country, including me and Ida, wanted to put the murderers in jail.

But Sam assumed that I knew about his gangster life. That's what he'd meant by "us". In those days, during Prohibition, "us" meant people in the liquor trade.

"Sam, do you think this one person, this Hoover, will be in charge of stopping all the bootleggers? All the gangsters? He could never do it!"

Sam looked at me and, for the first time, I saw a hardness in him. His eyes narrowed and I sensed that he might be about to lose his temper. I guess I looked alarmed. As if he was reminding himself that we were friends, he smiled.

9

Then he said, "You're right. People want the shooting stopped, but most of them don't mind the bootlegging and the speakeasies. But here's the thing, if some idiots shoot each other in Chicago, there are people in Chicago making money off the rackets, aldermen and cops and judges and politicians, and even other bootleggers, who will put a stop to it. Why? Because the headlines create too much attention. And once they shine the light, you never know who's going to be seen. The politicians and the cops are more interested in getting these *schmendricks* to behave than anybody."

"Sam," I said, really loud, "You're talking about blackmailing a government official!"

"Absolutely nothing wrong with taking pictures," Sam parried. "Just take the pictures. You won't be breaking any laws that I know of. Forget about everything else. Forget you ever even heard this guy's name. If maybe, somehow, I happen to get hold of these pictures, what I do is my responsibility, not yours. "

Somehow, that didn't seem true. If I know that pictures I take are going to be used for blackmail, against a Federal official no less, I'm surely guilty of *something*. Sam's idea was crazy, dangerous. I was trying to think of a way to refuse him when he said, "Al, you can name your price."

"I don't know, Sam. I've never done anything like this before. It sounds really dangerous. I could lose everything. I don't want to go to jail. I certainly don't want to be deported back to Ungvar!"

10

"Al, I promise you, I'll keep you safe. I'll keep you out of it."

So, thinking that I was humoring him, lying to myself, I said, "I wouldn't know what to charge you, Sam. Let me think it over." Ida had said that I shouldn't make any decisions until I talked it over with her. I'd use her as an excuse. My idea was to go back and have Ida tell me the whole idea was insane, so I could tell Sam that his cousin had a conniption and issued a marital veto.

He looked at his wristwatch and said, "Let me take you out to a nice dinner. We'll talk it over, work something out. I happen to own half of a terrific place just off The Boardwalk. Let me show you a good time. What do you say?"

"A good time sounds like a good idea." I said. I saw no harm in a fine meal.

Sam picked up the desk telephone and spoke to the switchboard operator. "Yeah, tell Lou we're going to walk over to *Babette's*. We're leaving in five minutes."

When the elevator arrived, out walked the strongman who'd brought me upstairs. Sam introduced him as Lou Kessel, the house detective.

"Mr. Rubin," said Louie with that husky Russian voice. "Pleasure to make your acquaintance."

"Likewise."

Sam said, "Wait 'til you see *Babette's*. Some of the waiters are beautiful women. And I guarantee you the best *schnapps* this side of Scotland. And wait 'til you see

11

the bar in the saloon; it's the only one like it in the whole world."

Boss of Atlantic City

The entrance to *Babette's Bath and Turf Club* was under a red neon sign a couple of blocks from the hotel. The guys I'd seen hanging out in the lobby when I'd checked in came with us as we walked: one ahead and one behind.

As we were taking off our coats inside the club, Sam apologized. "Believe me, Al, I'm not used to needing bodyguards. It's because nobody knows who killed A.R.. When we find out, I'll maybe feel safe again."

"So, it's true. You knew Arnold Rothstein."

"Sure I knew him. We were close, good friends, even though he was much older, even older than you. He took me under his wing, as they say, opened lots of doors for me. I tell you, I don't know what this world's coming to. Him getting killed, especially like that, all alone in a cheap hotel room, was awful. He was not a violent man, you know. He hated it when people got hurt. And he was straight with everyone, not the type of person to cross anybody. It was probably just one guy who did it, an individual, who maybe got in too deep at Saratoga or one of A.R.'s casinos. But the man should have had a bodyguard, what with all the people who owed him money."

A pretty woman in a low-cut dress with sequins on it greeted Sam by name. They seemed to be very good friends. He called her, "Babs."

"I'm Babette Stebbins," she said. I shook her hand and tried not to stare down her dress. The gal who took our coats was wearing one of those flapper outfits, with a hem way above the knee, the kind of dress I absolutely would not have allowed Helen or Pauline to even think about.

The saloon, as Sam had promised, was unique – the top parts of a cabin cruiser dominated the room, its white hull cut down at the waterline so that the boat appeared as if it was sailing on the blue-painted floor. The name of the boat, "*Babs*," was in ornate, gold script on the prow. Customers lined up on stools around the outside, in the water, as it were. Inside the rail, as if they were standing on the deck, a crew of busy bartenders in sailor uniforms pulled booze from shelves where a wheelhouse ought to have been. When Sam and I sat, a bartender actually saluted him, as if Sam Brodsky was the captain of the bar. I said I'd drink whatever Sam was having.

During Prohibition, once every month or so, I bought a bottle of blended bootleg whiskey, pretty good stuff, from a guy down the street. I kept it in the kitchen cupboard, over the sink. Most nights, when I came up from the studio, I knocked back a shot.

Sam told the bartender to bring twelve-year old scotch. It didn't taste like anything I'd ever had. I kind of choked, the aroma was so strong. I realized you had to sip it. By the third sip, I was liking it.

"Sam," I said, "This isn't a speakeasy, it's a wide-open saloon! Isn't there even a make-pretend Prohibition in Atlantic City?"

"Nope," Sam smiled. "Every cop, every fireman, every city official in Atlantic City works for Nucky Johnson. Most of the hotel and restaurant workers owe their jobs to Nucky. Nucky's the boss. You know who Nucky is?"

"I've seen his name in the papers. He's Enoch Johnson? City Treasurer or something?"

"Right. Enoch, that's Nucky. Nucky's the guy they call the Czar. Nucky controls everything that happens in Atlantic City. Everything. And Prohibition is working exactly the way he wants it to. There's no make-pretend about it."

"What about the Federal Government in Washington? Surely he has to listen to the Federal Government?"

"That's why Nucky and I are interested in getting something on Hoover and the Federals. State, local – hardly ever a problem – everybody wins. But Federal is different, especially this Hoover. But it's really hard to deal with the Federal people once they get involved. This Hoover guy is out to make a big name for himself, even if the people he's coming after are giving Americans exactly what they want. We think that once he sticks his nose into our business, he'll do what he did with the immigrants. There will be arrests by the hundreds, maybe even thousands; he'll call everybody a criminal, throw them in jail, and deport anybody who wasn't born here."

Babs came over and said that the table was ready. Sequins shimmered on her swaying *tush* as she led us to a corner table in the dining room. As we were sitting down, she said, "Do you want me to tell Nucky that you're here when he comes in?"

"Yeah," Sam said. "He wants to meet Al."

Sam went on about Prohibition. "You have to understand about the cops," he said. "They work for the politicians. The politicians in the State Capitol, Trenton, and especially the ones in Washington, are in Nucky's pocket."

"Seriously? You mean he pays them?"

"Maybe. That's Nucky's business, so I don't ask. But here's what I do know. In New Jersey, Nucky delivers Atlantic City, 90% Republican every damn election. Big turnouts. He's got the most reliable machine in the state. If you're a Republican, and you want to win a statewide election in New Jersey, you absolutely have to be a friend of Nucky Johnson's. There's no way to win without him. It hasn't been done since before the War. So that means that Senators and Congressmen, even Presidents, leave him alone. But it's not much different in other places. Why don't they close down the speakeasies in Philadelphia?"

"Well, I guess they're trying." I said. He looked at me as if I was a greenhorn, like I'd just gotten off the boat and I was still looking for gold cobblestones. "Well, probably not," I said.

"Definitely not. Some important people really like Prohibition because it's making them rich, not because of any Percy Van Bluenose, let me tell you. They like it because they get nice payoffs from guys like me to leave the speakeasies alone. In towns like Philly and New York and Chicago, the whole country in fact, Prohibition has been the best thing that could have happened. Prohibition has made thousands of two bit politicians, and lots of cops a whole lot richer, Atlantic City being your prime example." He stopped himself, "Listen, Al, am I boring you with all this?"

For us back then, me and Ida and the girls, Atlantic City was a summer resort. We could afford whole weeks at rooming houses for Ida and our two, almost grown up daughters, to spend down the shore. I had to mind the store, so I didn't go down very much. Ida went down the shore with the girls for a couple of weeks every August. I had to stay at the studio, so I could only come on the weekends. We usually stayed at Saul Lipinski's boarding house on States Avenue. The girls loved the beach. And Ida, she'd loved getting all dressed up and going out on the Boardwalk at night. She sees all her friends and they talk and talk and talk; it's a *yenta* convention, an awful business that the men did anything to avoid. The women sat in the rolling chairs parked by the railing and we, the men, had to drag them back to the rooming houses. Our girls, Helen and Pauline, they met their friends there, too.

I said, "For us, Atlantic City is a family place, where you take your wife and kids to get out of the heat, enjoy the seashore, you know?"

He nodded, understanding. "For me, it's business. Everybody I know, from all over the country, comes to Atlantic City. It's safe here. You know what it's like? You know how they have the League of Nations in Switzerland? Well, that's Atlantic City."

A Negro in a starched white jacket came to the table holding silver-domed trays aloft with either hand. I had let Sam order for me. At the entrance, where Babs had greeted us, I'd noticed a mural of a Chinese fisherman with a lantern in a little boat, so I had been assuming that Babette's was a Chinese restaurant until I saw the menu, which was in French. So this is *chateaubriand*, I thought when the waiter whisked the silver dome off my plate. It looked like roast beef to me.

"Is it cooked?" I asked. Ida never allows anything pink on my plate.

"Just try it, Al. The chef will make it right if you don't like it."

Reluctantly, I took a tiny slice of the beef and was amazed.

Sam's mother and Ida's father were sister and brother from Grodno, Lithuania. Going to Sam's Bar Mitzvah in 1915 had been a huge inconvenience that I had tried hard

18

to avoid. But Ida had been adamant because her father, may he rest in peace, insisted that we go; family first. So we left the girls, they were just babies, with friends and took the train to Penn Station in New York on a Friday night and stayed in a hotel. The next morning, at a diner while we were at breakfast, we looked at the *Metropolitan Transit Authority* map. We took subways to a synagogue in the Bronx for the occasion of my wife's cousin's thirteenth birthday. It was the first time I met Sam Brodsky.

I had been impressed. He was a little guy, but so poised. Even though the Brodskys had been in America only six years, he spoke English without an accent, and his Hebrew was excellent; you could tell that he knew and understood exactly what that Saturday's portion of the Torah was about. Afterward, I watched him at the reception in the basement of the synagogue. His friends were deferential, speaking quietly, listening carefully to him. He'd worn a suit of beautiful, soft worsted, a blue silk tie, and fine leather shoes. His parents were also very well turned out. I remember wondering how Max Brodsky, Sam's father, a pants cutter who worked in a sweatshop, could afford such clothes.

Phony pride is to be expected from parents at such occasions. But there was nothing phony about Max and Yetta's attitude. They were more than proud. Sam was somebody special and it was obvious to everyone.

Over the years, Sam and I talked at other Bar Mitz-vahs, and at funerals, and at weddings. Even though I was seventeen years older, we had become friends. We'd find each other at the gatherings and share cigarettes in quiet corners. We'd talk about baseball and politics and family, just the usual. But we liked each other. From the begin-ning, until that night at Babette's, I hadn't asked Sam how he made his money. He had decided, apparently, that I should know.

"Everyplace else in America," he said, "Has factories and stores and houses and like that. Here, most all the houses are for the hotel and restaurant workers, mostly Negroes. There's a neighborhood for the Italians who do the construction and the hauling and like that. The Jews here in town, like most places, have little stores. Hardly anybody lives in this town who isn't connected with tak-ing care of the visitor, giving people what they want."

"Myself," I said, "I'd love to have a studio on the Boardwalk where people stick their heads in cut-out holes for souvenir pictures of their vacation. There's already a couple on The Boardwalk and they seem to do alright. But I think the leases are hard to come by, you have to know somebody. Right?"

"Are you serious?" Sam asked, leaning toward me. "Because if that's what you want I'm sure I could get you a lease."

"Well, it's something I've been thinking about. I know that I can't afford it right now. I'm still paying off my equipment in Philadelphia."

A blonde woman in a black dress that was held up by one, thin strap brought us another round of scotch. When she left, Sam leaned across the table. "Listen, Al, there's no other place like Atlantic City for making money. The convention business has gone crazy since Prohibition. Every Tom, Dick and Harry wants his association to have the annual meeting right here in Atlantic City. Why? Because there's no Prohibition! The booze is what loosens them up. After the dumb speeches are over, the conventions are all about sex and gambling. These men walk a block or two inland and find whatever they want. I mean everybody can find what he wants here, no matter how strange. And, Al, we're not just talking about the East Overshoe Moose Lodge. We're talking about the biggest outfits, like the steel, and the railroads, and the car companies. It's a year-round, off-the-Boardwalk operation."

"But you're right, the summer's great for family stuff. The right Boardwalk businesses do more than enough income to last the year. So, let's say I could get you a lease for a studio on the Boardwalk for souvenir pictures. You could close your shop in Philly every summer and you and Ida could spend the whole season down here. I'll even pay the first year's rent. What do you say?"

I was stunned. "Sam, that's too generous. I could never accept that."

"Not at all." He leaned away from the table and sipped his scotch. "It would be a pleasure to help family and, believe me, I'd be getting something from you of great value to me. I'd definitely be getting the better end of the deal. Your conscience would be clear. How can either of us go wrong?"

"What if Hoover doesn't show? Or if I can't get a shot? What then?"

"No matter," he said. "I trust you to do whatever's humanly possible. Picture or no picture, as long as you give it your all, the lease is yours."

That's when Nucky Johnson came into *Babette's Bath and Turf Club*. Looking across the dining room toward the saloon, I saw a tall, imposing man with slick, dark hair. Standing next to him, handing their coats to Babs, was Lou Kessel.

Sam said "There's the czar himself. That's Nucky Johnson."

"And Lou Kessel works for him?"

"Louie is his number one, always within shouting distance, usually a lot closer. He even cooks Nucky's breakfast." I must have seemed skeptical. Sam said, "Seriously, Louie cooks his breakfast. I've seen it. Of course, Nucky's not usually out of bed until four in the afternoon."

I watched a procession approach Nucky and Lou at the boat-shaped bar. Lou took an envelope from one guy and slid it into his jacket. A few minutes later, a man was talking to Nucky with great intensity. I watched the czar peel bills off a wad of cash and place them in the man's hand. As the man thanked him, Nucky raised his palms and shrugged. The supplicant backed away to make room for another. Nucky towered over the throng, wearing a red carnation on the silk-piped lapel of his dinner jacket.

Sam twisted around in his chair to watch. I was wishing that there was color photography. I didn't usually go in for tinting photos; I'd do it if a customer insisted. But Nucky's carnation was just too good to leave gray.

As we were watching, the table got cleared. The bare-shouldered blonde was serving us brandy in huge snifters when Babs led Nucky and Lou through the arch into the dining room and to our table. Sam rose to shake Nucky's hand. He was shorter than the Czar by more than a foot.

"Nucky," said Sam, "Let me introduce you to a very dear friend of mine. Al Rubin, from Philadelphia, meet Nucky Johnson."

Nucky took my hand in his. He said, "It's a pleasure. And this is my friend, Lou Kessel."

"We've met," Louie said. Then he walked toward the bar, stopped, and turned around near the archway. Indeed, he was within shouting distance.

Nucky pulled a chair from another table and sat down. "Babs, bring me a Will Rogers. You've got a nice crowd here tonight," he said, surveying the room.

"It's mostly the Elks from Michigan, I think." said Sam. "They came in this afternoon. And there's some kind of doctors' conference, too. But, yeah, it's a good crowd. After dinner, me and Al are going to check upstairs and see how the casino's doing."

"With you, Sam, it's always fine." The tall man directed his attention to me. "Did you know your friend Sam is a genius?" he asks. I didn't say anything. What kind of genius? "Let me tell you," Nucky reiterated, "He's a genius."

He and Sam started talking business. I tried to follow, but it was hard. I watched the people in the restaurant, particularly the lady waiters. With half an ear, I heard them talk about people I didn't know. Once or twice, I saw men head toward our table only to be cut off by the vigilant Louie Kessel.

Then Sam said, "Al here is looking to have one of those picture taking places on the Boardwalk. He's got a studio in Philly and he's looking to branch out. What do you think?"

"It's not a bad idea," said the Czar. "Those places seem to do good business. Do you have a location in mind?"

Where indeed? I'd actually thought about it. I thought that the pier locations were the best. In the seconds I pondered Nucky's question, a dozen summer nights flashed through my head. To me, The Boardwalk was a carnival, it was Broadway, it was the biggest and loudest of state fairs. If you had the stamina, you could walk the four mile length in one night.

The great entertainment piers were perpendicular to the Boardwalk, extending over the sand into the surf. They had theatres, sideshows, midways, Ferris wheels, merry-go-rounds, thrill rides, even little museums and curiosity booths. They had carnie barkers and hucksters, just like the rest of the Boardwalk. On rainy days, people lined up for the three-a-day vaudeville shows. The ball-rooms were packed every night with people dancing to radio bands like Paul Whiteman's and Red Nichols'. Ida loved to dance.

So during the day there was the steady trade - people who, for one reason or another, had had enough of sand and sea. Sunburn, maybe. But the big crowds were at night. The bonus payoff was on the rainy days when beach people needed somewhere to go.

Sitting around the white linen and heavy silverware with Sam and Nucky, I imagined customers waiting in line, dollar bills in hand, as the rain pattered on the roof of my studio. They all wanted to poke their faces through my beautiful painting with the lettering, "Atlantic City – Queen of Resorts."

I should have said 'no thank you.' Or I should, po-litely, have said, 'I need to think it over, to look at my choices, to discuss it with my accountant.' But I didn't. Out came, "*Steel Pier, Million Dollar Pier, Ocean Pier*. Any of them would be good. I guess *Steel Pier* would be my first choice."

Nucky said, "Okay, I'll talk to George Hamid. He'll help you out. Sam knows how to get in touch with you?"

Sam said, "Call me when George is ready to sit down and Al and I will take care of it. Thanks, Nucky."

The Treasurer of Atlantic County New Jersey stood up. "Alright, gentlemen. I've got to get over to Arctic Avenue, some friends are waiting. Sam, good to see you. Al, It's a pleasure to make your acquaintance."

Casino Mirror

I told Sam that I was not a gambling man, but after dinner he took me upstairs at *Babette's* just to show off his casino. It turned out that the mural of the Chinese fisherman was a false wall that functioned as a doorway hiding an elevator and a stairway to the second floor. We took the stairs.

The casino was an open room as big as an auditorium. People were rolling dice down long green tables and hollering, and they were standing around a roulette wheel and hollering, and they were playing cards, quietly, at big round tables. A row of machines was lined up against a wall. People were putting coins into slots and pulling handles. Sam said they were called slot machines and that people are crazy for them. "Go figure," he said..

The sound of the machines was peculiarly inviting; I liked the thrumming of spinning gears, the way the bicycle bell sounded, the happy tinkling of the pennies falling into the steel dishes. The air was thick with tobacco smoke. Through the haze I saw a bar at the far end of the room where a guy was serving drinks to pretty women who carried them on trays to the people at the tables.

27

It was late, and I was tired. I was supposed to call Ida to make sure she didn't wait up for me. I should have gone home, but I didn't want to leave. The room pulled at me − I wanted to gamble, even though I didn't know how.

Sam started walking away. "Al, enjoy yourself. I've got to check on a few things."

I said, "Sam, I have to call Philadelphia and tell Ida for sure that I'll be staying at the *Ritz*." So Sam snapped his fingers at this guy who just seemed to be standing around. He said, "Wally, take Mr. Rubin into the office so he can make the phone call. See you later, Al," he said. "Have a little fun."

Wally led me through a door that I could barely see because it was covered with the wallpaper. We were in a hallway. Wally opened another door and stuck his head in and said to someone inside, "Mr. Brodsky says this guy can use the phone."

I walked into a room that was barely lit. A fellow was sitting in front of a window with a view of the casino, his back to me. The phone was on the desk, but I was captivated by the man at the window. I recognized him, an old friend named Mike Finnerty.

When I first met Mike, it was right after I bought my building. He was making his way by doing odd jobs in the neighborhood. He worked cheap and I'd needed help. We worked side-by- side whenever I needed another pair of hands to build something in the studio. At first, we'd

been "Mr. Rubin" and "Mr. Finnerty." Then we'd share
a beer or two after the projects were finished. Then we'd
share a beer or two just because we liked each other's
company.

He had secrets. Mike wouldn't tell you what ship
brought him to America. If you asked him about Ireland,
or his arrival, or his family, he went quiet. He'd come
over from Ireland eight years before, in 1921, when people were shooting each other during the fight to make the
East part of the new Republic of Ireland. It was a bloody
civil war, in the papers all the time, Catholics and
Protestants killing each other every day.

Though Michael never said so, I believed he'd been
smuggled into America. Since the day I'd met him, I had
assumed that he'd been mixed up with the fighting and
that he was in hiding from the English. His hatred for the
English was always near the surface, ready to flare.

There was probably no better place for such a person
to get lost than Southwest Philadelphia. It seemed that
half of Eyre lived in sight of the twin bell towers of the
Church of the Most Blessed Sacrament at 56th Street and
Chester Avenue, a block from my studio. I did a terrific
business in Holy Communion pictures.

It was only a couple of years later that Mike stopped
doing the odd jobs, moved into a much bigger apartment,
and bought a car. He was never specific, but said he was
working for some "fellers from New York." It was Mike
who'd supplied us with the bottled beer that we drank. In

1927, he left the neighborhood to take a good job down the shore, and we lost touch.

But there he was, wearing a suit and working in an office. We shook hands. We hugged and patted each other's back.

I asked, "What are *you* doing *here*?"

"I work for Mr. Brodsky, Al. I watch out for his interests here at the casino, don't you know. Are you friendly with Mr. Brodsky, Al?"

I said, "Yeah, he's Ida's cousin. And a friend, too."

"Sam's me boss, Al. Your cousin's me boss." I realized that I'd missed his brogue.

There was a phone on the desk. Before I asked how he comes to know a Jewish gangster from New York, I had to call home. He turned to watch the casino as the operator made the connection to Philadelphia. I told Ida I was going to spend the night, and she said she was disappointed, and how did it go with Sam? "What's the deal?" she asked. I said I'd tell her when I got home, but she wanted to know more. She wanted to know, "Are you going to do it? Whatever it is?"

So I changed the subject and said, "Guess who works for Sam?" We talked for a minute about Mike, who knew our kitchen well. He had a bottomless appetite for Ida's Hungarian apple strudel. She liked inviting "that poor bachelor" to have coffee and dessert at our table so that she could listen to his blarney as he ate. "It's delicious, Ida. Better and better every time. And it smells so

good, Ida! Ohh, Albert, you're a twicet lucky man; oncet
to have Ida for your wife and second to have me for your
friend. Because if I'm not your true friend I'm stealin'
her away, so fine and extra-ordinary a woman as herself.
And isn't she too good for you?" Ida loved it.

The long distance operator connected me to our
apartment over the studio. I told Ida that we'd talk about
Sam's idea when I returned the next day. If I was to be
late, she'd open up the studio without me. "Okay," she
said, and we hung up.

There was something strange about the window. I figured it out when a lady came by and looked in. I saw that
she thought it was a mirror because she touched her hair
and straightened the strap on her dress. It was the first
one-way mirror I'd ever seen and it gave me an idea of
how I could take a picture of Hoover.

Mike kept his eye on the window as we caught up. We
talked about people who had stores on the Avenue near
my studio. He asked about some of the pretty girls he
used to squire around in his *Reo* convertible.

I saw Sam make his way through the casino toward
the office. When he came in, he was taken aback by the
silly grins that Mike and I were wearing. I said, "Guess
what, Sam?" And I explained that Mike Finnerty and Al
Rubin were old friends.

He looked from Mike to me a couple of times and
shook his head. "Go figure," he said.

31

Mike, looking through the window, raised his hand and said, "Hold on. Hold on. Sam, I've got to go." He hurried out of the office.

Through the glass, we watched him collect Wally, the fellow that Sam had sent to open the office for me. We saw them huddle for a moment. Then Wally walked to the roulette table and grabbed one of the gamblers by the arm. Wally said something in his ear and the guy tried to act as if a large man didn't have one hand on his bicep and the other on his collar. They backed away from the table and headed toward the office.

Then I saw that Mike was taking long strides to catch up with a woman in a hurry to get to the stairway. He grabbed her arm just as she was about to go down. She started to pull away from him. He leaned way down to say something to her. She went pale, wide-eyed. I felt sorry for her.

I glanced over at Sam. He was glowering. Out the window, it was business as usual; people were so intent on their games that the little dramas were going unnoticed.

Wally burst in with the man from the roulette table. Then Mike came in with the woman. She cowered, as if she expected to be hurt. It was suddenly very crowded in the office.

"Smooth. Very nice," said Sam. "What were they doing?"

"Dipping, I do believe," said Mike. "Go ahead, Darlin', let's see what's down your dress."

The second that Mike let go of her, she tried to break for the door. He grabbed her again, this time holding both her arms from behind. She was crying, protesting, saying who are we to treat her so. The man, still in Wally's grasp, had stopped struggling. Mike said, "Sam, me hands are full. She's got the swag on her somewhere."

Sam went to the woman and patted the bosom of her black dress. He undid the one rhinestone button that was over her chest bone, reached inside, and pulled out a man's wallet. He put that on the desk, reached in again and brought out a necklace. He cocked his head and stared at the woman. She raised her chin. Sam said, "Al, why don't you wait for me at the bar. Get yourself a drink."

I grabbed the door handle as quickly as I could and left the office. The door was closing behind me as I heard the man speak up. "Please mister," he said, "Don't hurt us." My heart was pounding. I took a couple of steps in the hallway and turned around. I started to reopen the door to say goodbye to Mike, then I yanked it closed. In the split second, through the inch of reopened doorway, I saw Mike holding the woman's arms as Sam swung his open hand to slap her face.

Back in the casino, I leaned against the wall between the mirror and the wallpapered door for a moment to

33

catch my breath. My heart was still pounding. I headed across the room to wait for Sam at the bar.

He emerged after a couple of long minutes, inspected the cuffs of his shirt, lit a cigarette, and made his way between the tables toward me. He sat down on the stool next to mine, as calm as ever I'd seen him, not a slicked hair out of place. He asked for seltzer with ice and a shot of scotch.

"I can't get over people like that," he said to me. "I hope they spread the word. Thieves! *Goniffs*! How's the booze, Al? Didn't I tell you it's great *schnapps*? The best, right?"

So, I knew. I knew.

A Lot to Lose

I felt like a million bucks the next morning – a big shot.
There I was, driving the *De Soto* through the gloomy
Pine Barrens, past the fields, past the bare trees of the
peach orchards, with my own personal heater to keep me
warm. Going through the towns, stopping at the lights, I
imagined every pedestrian as one of the thousands of customers who would happily pay a dollar for Atlantic City
souvenir photos.

With that much money I would send both girls to
Normal School, or perhaps even to a regular, four-year
college. I would pay off the bank loans. I would bring
Ida's sisters, their husbands and their kids over from Ruthenia. I would buy a house and collect rent on the apartment over the studio. And, of course, I pictured all of this
happening as Ida and I enjoyed good seats at the *Acade-
my of Music*, oil paintings, bronze statues and fine furniture. I was rehearsing ways to persuade Ida that we
should accept Sam's offer as I crossed the Delaware River Bridge coming in to Philadelphia from Camden.

I parked on 55th Street and grabbed my suitcase from
the trunk. I saw that Ida had turned on the lights and unlocked the door of *Albert Photographic Studio*. She
looked up from sorting through the envelopes returned

35

from the lab and said, "It's about time. What happened to 'I'll be home in time to open up' ?"

"Nice hello you give your husband after a hard business trip," I said. She hugged me back and kissed my cheek. "I should feel sorry for you?" she mocked. "At the *Ritz*? A dinner for free? Poor Al."

I went upstairs to put on a clean collar and tie and make myself a cup of coffee. I returned to the studio on the back stairs, remembering that the first job Mike had helped me with was building the partition that shields the stairway from the trade. We had done a good job.

I started out with the best part. I said, "Sam says he can get us a lease for a souvenir photo stall on *Steel Pier*. It's not difficult for him, he says. And he's offered to pay the whole first year's rent. How does that sound?"

"To do what? Rob a bank?" Ida said.

I recall that it was an unusually busy day, we had to take care of the trade, so It took most of the day to tell her everything and to answer her questions. Usually, on a weekday, business was slow until people came home from work on the trolley and dropped off film or picked up their negatives and prints. We used a big lab downtown.

That April day was a little busier than normal, because Mr. and Mrs. Fishman came in at 10 o'clock for their fiftieth anniversary portrait. Cy, their son, who had the haberdashery across the street, was paying for it. At one o'clock, Father Duffy, who was retiring as principal of

Roman Catholic High School, came in to sit for the color-tinted portrait that was going to be hung in the marble hallway outside the school office. In between, the sleigh bells attached to the door jingled steadily with other customers. Some of them wanted to look at the sample albums. Most were dropping off or picking up lab jobs.

By the time Ida went upstairs at two o'clock, she'd heard it all except for the part about the pickpockets in the casino. She was being the sensible one, the thoughtful one — I couldn't tell how she felt about the idea.

At three thirty, Pauline came home from West Philadelphia High School. "Hi, Pop," she said, on her way upstairs. Twenty minutes later, after she'd changed out of her school dress and eaten the plate of cookies that she had every day, she breezed back through. "Bye, Pop," she said on her way out the front door. She was on her way to *Yudelson's Drug Store*, a block away, to sit and talk with her friends. The soda fountain always paid for Mrs. Yudelson's next mink coat.

Pauline wanted a lot. She wanted to wear makeup. She wanted new clothes. She wanted me to buy a new car. She wanted us to eat in restaurants. She wanted all of the other girls to like her. She wanted a boyfriend. She wanted so much that she was disappointed a lot of the time. As the door closed behind her, I decided that we would have a conversation at the dinner table and talk about the important things in life, the things money can't buy.

Her sister Helen, three years older, came home from her job at around five thirty. She worked in the office of a candy factory. While I emptied the cash register into the *Corn Exchange Bank* bag and wrote the deposit slip, Helen swept the floor, put albums where they belonged on the display shelves, and made sure that the sample pictures on the walls were hanging straight. I put all of the customer film into the pick-up bag for the lab's delivery man who would come first thing the following morning. As we did this, Helen told me about her day at the candy factory. "It's too easy," she said. Most of her job involved filing invoices and receipts. I hung the "Closed" sign on the door, locked it, and turned off the lights.

Upstairs, Pauline was in the kitchen with Ida. Apparently, she'd come home through the back door. I assumed she was avoiding me. Ida was saying, "We'll go over to *Isenberg's* and pick out the pattern when you come home from school tomorrow. We can use that nice cotton print that I used for Helen's. I've got plenty."

"Can't I have something else?" Pauline whined.

"What's wrong with the print? It's so pretty. You love it, you said."

I poured myself a shot from the bottle that I kept over the sink, knocked it back, rinsed my glass, and closed the cabinet.

Pauline said, "But what if me and Helen are together? We'll look like the Bobbsey Twins. Please, Ma, let me pick out some new fabric."

As I left the kitchen to get my house slippers, Ida was saying, "Alright, alright. Maybe I'll make myself something with the print. I could use another dress to wear downstairs."

At the table, as we had supper, I said that nice clothes are not that important. "What's important is if you're a good person." Pauline nodded, but I could tell that her mind was on something else. Helen asked where I went last night. I said that I went to Atlantic City to see about opening up a studio on the Boardwalk. Both girls thought it was a wonderful idea.

After supper, Helen sat at the piano to practice as I read the newspaper in my chair. I liked the *Bulletin*, although there weren't enough articles about Europe. After awhile, Ida went into her sewing room.

Pauline had homework to do in her room.

Helen worked on a Chopin waltz for an hour or so before she went off to her room. Finally, Ida and I could continue our conversation about Sam's offer.

I went into the sewing room. "Tell me more about this Hoover person," she said. "He doesn't sound like a somebody that you want to have mad at you."

"I don't know anything about him," I replied. "I never even heard of him until yesterday."

"Well I think you should find out. Sam may not be telling you everything. If he's a good man, I don't know that you should even get involved. Sam might think he's a terrible person, but we both know that Sam is not necessarily a good judge of such things. It's like you were telling Pauline at supper, Sam is one of those who puts money first. I'm not sure I want to trust him."

I didn't want to understand her; I had been completely seduced. "Whether or not John Hoover is a good man, I don't know. I can live with taking a picture so long as that's all I have to do. If he doesn't do anything to be ashamed of, it doesn't matter. If he does do bad things and I take his picture, then he isn't such a good man. Besides, Sam says that taking a picture isn't against the law. I'll obey the law. My conscience will only be a little bit bothered."

I was picturing Reb Mendel, with his arms crossed under his beard and one eyebrow raised, as I explained my reasoning about the photographs to Ida. I had attended *cheder* during my childhood in Ungvar, a city in Hungary. Reb Mendel led discussions with the older boys and the men, framing questions about what's right and wrong and what the Torah and the Talmud have to say about it. We little ones were supposed to be working on our Hebrew, but I liked the grownup conversations.

Ida said, "Do me the favor of finding out a little, just to make sure that this Hoover person is who Sam says he is. Maybe you should talk to a lawyer about taking the pictures, too."

"That I will not do. Who would I ask? Should I ask Officer Mulroney? Should I ask that shyster Leventhal?

Please, Ida. This will have to stay our business." Then I
explained what really worried me.

"I don't know whether to use film or wet plate. Either
way, how can I make it sensitive enough? The pictures
will be blurry if Hoover moves at all unless I can make
either the film or the glass emulsion super sensitive. I
think it can be done, but I don't know how."

"So, how could you find out?"

"I guess I could write to Kodak. They probably know,
but they may not want to tell me. We'll see. That's only
part of the problem. How am I going to hide the camera?"

Ida folded up the fabric she was working on and
switched off the sewing machine light bulb. "Sam actually promised to pay the whole first year's rent?"

"He did," I said.

"*Steel Pier*?"

"*Steel Pier*."

"You'll have to be very, very careful," she said, looking me in the eye.

We stared at each other.

Finally, I said, "Ida, I will take every precaution. If I
can't do it safely, I won't do it at all."

She stepped into my embrace and I rested my chin on
her head, thinking that I had a lot to lose, not just a lot to
gain.

Latest Equipment

I figured that Hermann Spiedecker was as likely to
know about low-light photography as anyone. Because
I didn't go to his place very often, I got lost in the smoky
maze of North Philadelphia's industrial district; one cob-
blestone street of row houses is a lot like the others. The
block-long factories were a little different from each other out front, with nice signs and fancy entrances. In back,
the loading docks and railroad sidings all looked alike.
Finally, after aiming the *De Soto* over trolley tracks and
around trucks and horse-drawn wagons, I saw the *G&H*
sign in an alley off of Diamond Street near 10th. The
chemical smell was so strong when I walked through the
front door that it almost knocked me back outside.

When I first knew Hermann, back during the Great
War, when he and his brother Gunther were starting the
business, he used to have a thick head of blond hair. In
1929, he had hardly any hair. We were good friends who
hadn't seen each other in many years, though we talked
often over the telephone about business. I had called
about light sensitivity. He said he could solve my problem.

"When was the last time, Al?" Hermann asked me as
we stood in a hallway by a door with a red light bulb

glowing over it. He was wearing a rubber apron and peel-ing off elbow-length rubber gloves. Most conversations with Hermann happened when he was doing something else.

"Honest, Hermann, I don't remember. Was it the time we all went to the Orchestra? You and Hazel, me and Ida? They did a Tchaikovsky thing?"

"*Ya!* That's it," he said. "Too long. Too long." So we agreed that we should do something about it, but we knew we wouldn't because we had drifted into different circles over the years. No matter, we were still friends, and we did good business together.

"What do you hear from Gunther?" I asked as we walked down the hallway. The older brother had returned to Germany after the War, selling his share of the lab back to Hermann. I was never told the reason he left. Gunther wasn't a friendly sort of person, so I hadn't known him nearly as well as Hermann. I do remember him being angry at the anti-German propaganda posters and newspaper articles.

"Gunther's doing okay, I guess. I get a letter every couple of months. Still single. He's working for *Farben* at the chemical works in Munich. He's joined some sort of political club that he seems real excited about."

"Good for him," I said.

"So why are you so interested in sensitizing film?"

I was ready for that. I said, "I think there's money to be made in candid photography. Don't you?"

"*Ya*, absolutely," my friend said. "But mostly by me and the portable camera manufacturers. How are you going to make money out of candid shots in a studio?"

Hermann was smart, and I didn't want to lie, so I just said, "I have a few ideas. I want to know if it can be done before I go to too much trouble."

"What camera are you going to use?"

For the Hoover pictures, on the day I showed up at Hermann's lab, I had been planning to use film sheets in the latest *Graflex*. At the time, I still liked using glass plates for studio portraits because the grain is finer. But glass weighs so much and is really too fragile for outside work. I had not yet made the switch to rolled film, because I hadn't found a reliable camera with lenses that I thought were suitable for commercial portraits. I was even using the *Graflex* for the high school graduation pictures, even though I had to *schlep* cases filled with four-by-five inch film holders into gymnasiums.

"I'll use the new *Graflex*, the *Speed Graphic* model. I can fit it with a 2.8 lens, very fast. *Zeiss* makes one for the *Graflex*."

He looked at me with a skeptical expression. "Okay," he said. "I'll tell you what I know." We were in his office. He hung up his apron and picked up a pile of mail from his desktop and carried it to the window where he started reading the envelopes.

"I know two things you can do, *ya?,* that will at least double the sensitivity. The first one is heat up a dish of

45

mercury in the darkroom and leave the film there. The mercury vapor reacts with the silver halide crystals in the film emulsion. If you expose the film to mercury vapor, the emulsion will have more than twice the sensitivity it had when you started. Leave the film there overnight. After that, the reaction is over, and no more sensitivity happens to the emulsion. The problem is that it will wear off. Maybe after a week or ten days, *ya?,* the film is what it used to be, even maybe a little less."

That will work, I thought. I would expose the film to the mercury vapor just before Decoration Day.

"But don't be in the room with the mercury vapor. You don't have to heat it very hot, the vapor will come off with little more heat than from a candle flame. But it's poison. *Ya?* "

"I've heard that hat makers are crazy because of mercury," I said.

"*Nein*, not really crazy. You know. How should I say it? *Die Demensz*? You know, *die Demensz*?" Sometimes I understand Hermann because Yiddish is so much like German. But not that time. He explained, "It's their brains get rotten in them from the fumes, *ya*? They bump into things like drunk people. Sometimes they see things that aren't there. And they lose memories."

"That's awful. What do hat makers use the mercury for?"

After he sorted the envelopes, he put them on the desk and sat to work on them with a letter opener that looked like a little saber. "It's the nitrate of mercury what they use. Very volatile. They put beaver skins in it. What do you call with the fur still on? Pelts, *ya*? Beaver pelts, or rabbit pelts, in vats of mercury nitrate, and the fur comes right of the skins. Then they grind up the fur, mix it with wool, and press it into huge, flat sheets. That's how they make the felt for hats. *Ya?"*

"Interesting," I said. Disgusting is what I thought.

"Ya, " he said, studying a bill.

"So, Hermann. What's this other way?"

"Ach!" he says. "This is a good one. This is a really good secret." He put down the mail and looked me in the eye. "All that is necessary is to pre-expose the plate or the film to a bright, white light source. That's all there is to it. Bring a light close to your lens, cover the lens with a white cloth, and pull the shutter. Use the same film over again, *ya?,* double exposure, and it will be a lot more sensitive." He looked at me, smiling, waiting for a reaction.

"Really?"

"Really. But, Albrecht, *mein gutter Freund,* why are you using film holders? So clumsy! You should use roll film now. It's much better. Look, I show you what Gunther sends me for Christmas. A *Rolleiflex*.You know the *Rolleiflex*?"

To be polite, I let Hermann demonstrate the light-weight camera that his brother sent him from Germany. I was impressed, deciding right then and there to use a *Rolleiflex* for the high school portraits. But I wasn't yet

47

sure that I wanted to risk using a new camera for Sam's special job.

As I was leaving *G&H*, I said, "Hermann, you are terrific to help me this way. Thanks a lot."

"Not a problem," he said. "Welcome to the 20th Century."

Trap

I had been sleeping in a suite on the fifth floor of the *Ritz Carlton* as I organized things in preparation for Decoration Day. Ida and the girls came to join me the first weekend in May. Ida and I had an appointment with a realtor to show us houses we might rent for the summer. On the Sunday morning, before we were to meet the agent, I took the elevator to the twelfth floor to inspect my handiwork, the result of weeks of work on adjoining suites with a crew from hotel maintenance and lots of Sam's money.

Even after all that effort and expense, I was pessimistic about the chances of the plan succeeding. As I said to Louie Kessel one day as we were working on the place, "Who does sex with the lights on? Who does sex unless they're under the covers?"

Lou said that Atlantic City is a place for secrets, a place where people let go. "After the beach, some people are same as Russian soldier on leave, all they think of is fucking, fucking, and fucking. You could be lucky, maybe Hoover is very sexed-up person like that."

Suite 1200 had been reserved for Hoover's stay on Decoration Day and the weekend following. I stood back from the living room mirror to make sure that the two peepholes situated behind the mirror frames couldn't be seen. I'd had normal mirrors built with frames made up of smaller, beveled mirrors. On each frame, there were two small squares of one-way mirror, one to conceal the camera peephole and one to conceal the peephole through which I would watch.

In the bedrooms, French doors opened to balconies that commanded a view of the Atlantic Ocean and of the beach for miles to the east and west. I hoped that my subjects would keep the curtain open. Why close it? The view was superb and no one except gulls could have seen inside.

I'd asked for a complete makeover of the rooms the FBI Director was going to occupy. All the furniture in Suite 1200 had been newly upholstered in shades of light tan, pale green, or white. A new white rug covered the floor, wall-to-wall. In the bedroom, the headboard was upholstered in white silk, the same fabric as the bed linens. Ten-bulb crystal chandeliers hung from both newly-painted white ceilings. We had put in as many table lamps and floor lamps as we could without having the place look like a lighting store. All the lamp shades were new, white silk. Everything was as I had ordered.

I left Suite 1200 and walked down the corridor to the door of what used to be Suite 1202, before I had the maintenance crew change the lettering on the corridor door to "Linens."

No one was in the corridor to see me open the door to a fake closet. I'd had the crew build a set of shelves on the back of the closet to disguise the door leading into into what used to be Suite 1202, the space I thought of as the blind.

I had experimented with Hermann's techniques by hanging rolls of unexposed film in the darkroom in Philadelphia. I'd used Ida's food warmer and lit a can of *Sterno* under a dish of mercury. I've always had an exhaust fan in the darkroom because, without strong ventilation, fumes from developing fluid gave me bad headaches. For the mercury experiment, I turned the fan off. The next morning, holding my breath, I went in for just a minute and turned the fan back on. An hour later, with the air cleared, I poured the mercury back into its bottle through a funnel. Then I spent a couple of hours rewinding the rolls and inserting them into a *Rolleiflex* camera.

In the studio, I created test rolls using different combinations of mercury enhancement and pre-exposure. To do the test exposures, I hung an ostrich-feather hat on a string and let it swing and twist in front of the *Rolleiflex* as I snapped frame after frame at different settings. Back in the darkroom I found out that Hermann had been right – pre-sensitized, mercury-enhanced film captures sharp images of moving objects in low light. The hardest part was rewinding the film back onto the spools.

In the blind, I had placed two *Rolleiflex* cameras on sturdy shelves, one behind each of the mirrors. Each of the cameras was precisely aimed and focused − one on the middle of the bed, the other on the sofa in the front room of the suite. I'd placed chairs next to both cameras. I'd installed velvet blackout drapes hanging down to the floor behind the cameras and over the chairs so that light would not leak through the mirrors into Hoover's suite. I thought I was ready. As Lou said, maybe I'd get lucky. Decoration Day was only weeks away.

Our appointment to look at rental houses was at nine o'clock. I locked the "linen closet" door and took the stairs down to the fifth floor, hoping to get the house tour over with as quickly as possible.

In our own suite, 504, the girls were playing cribbage on the floor of the living room. Ida was in the bedroom sitting with a copy of *Readers' Digest*. She popped up as I walked in. "Get your hat and coat," she said. "Your friend's real estate agent just this minute called from the lobby."

"I don't think he's exactly a real estate agent." I said.

"Then what is he? A gangster? A politician? What?"

I looked through the doorway at the girls. Did they hear the word "gangster?" I closed the door and spoke softly. "Ida. Please! I don't know much about him, except that he must be some kind of unusual character. Sam told me that Pace is doing this as a special favor to Nucky. Since Sam and Nucky are sort of partners, maybe that makes this Pace fellow a kind of partner too. Sam says we're very lucky to have Pace looking for us. He says nobody knows more about Atlantic City. Mike seems to have a different opinion. He just laughed when I told him that Peter Pace was going to help us out."

"So? What's so funny?"

"Ida. I don't know."

There was a knock. Pauline stuck her head in. "Mom," she said, "Can we go out instead of waiting here forever for you and Pop to look at houses?"

Ida nodded. "Okay. But stay together. And make sure you're back here by one o'clock. Where are you going?"

"Just out on The Boardwalk."

"But nothing is open yet."

"Maybe not," said Pauline. "But it beats sitting around playing cards."

So, we put on our coats and hats, and we all left together. I gave Helen the spare room key. "Remember, one o'clock. Not a minute later."

In the lobby, a skinny, white-haired man in his seventies sat on the edge of an armchair with a bowler hat perched on his kneecaps. He saw us as we came out of the elevator and unfolded himself. He was wearing high button shoes, the kind that most men threw out in favor of Oxfords before the Great War.

"I am Peter Pace," he said, grinning broadly. He handed me a business card that said he was an attorney with an office on Atlantic Avenue, the main street in the

53

business district. He worked my extended hand like a pump handle. After I introduced him to Ida, he bowed, extended his arm toward the Pacific Avenue doors and said, "Shall we get started?"

Waiting at the curb with its top down was a gleaming, blue *Duesenberg*. A young chauffeur wearing black livery stood waiting with one foot on the running board. He opened the back door and we all got in. "To the Inlet, William," said Pace. "Let's show these folks the house on Connecticut Avenue."

The *Doozey* glided away from the curb. As I leaned back in my seat, Ida reached over and squeezed my hand. I relaxed a little, thinking that being driven around a resort in a *Duesenberg* might not be such a bad way to spend a Sunday morning in May.

Summer Place

The *Doozey* had two back seats, Pace sat in the one that faced backward. Light wood paneling covered every surface but the carpeted floor. The leather upholstery was like a baby's *tush*. A cut crystal decanter and glasses were nestled in a bar mounted next to Pace's seat. Bud vases attached to the coachwork held fresh, red roses.

Pace spoke, "Even though I am long-since retired from daily participation in real estate, I do keep my eyes open and visit the offices regularly. I am happy, as a favor to Enoch, to show you around. Enoch said nothing of your requirements. Please tell me the kind of house you're looking for."

We told him about our family and that we wanted to rent a place that we might be able to buy after the season. We told him how much rent we could afford — maybe a hundred dollars a month.

"And you have a location in mind?" he asked.

Ida said, "Please, Mr. Pace, locations we're not too familiar with. Show us what you think is best."

He explained, "Atlantic City is built on a barrier island called Absecon. The island parallels the South Jersey coastline. Look at the map and you'll see that we are off that part of the coastline that curves inward, toward the Delaware Bay in an east-to-west orientation. Most of the western end of Absecon is unpopulated. The best properties, of course, are on the water. Those on the ocean side tend to be more desirable. Those on the Absecon Bay, somewhat less so. And the closer you are to the center of town, the railroad station, the better."

"You say the western end doesn't have people. Why is that?" Ida asked.

"Pestilence, ma'am. Pestilence," he said gravely. "Until not so long ago, nobody could live here, not even Indians. The marshes between the mainland and our famous sandy beach provide a breeding ground for mosquitoes, multitudes upon swarms. The greenhead fly, a very vicious insect, also loves the Absecon salt marsh."

Ida was looking alarmed. I patted her hand. "Don't worry. It's not a problem anymore. You can't afford to have such problems in a place like Atlantic City. Am I right, Mr. Pace?"

"Indeed." he said. "A solution to the insect problem is necessary if we are to continue in the resort business. As you are, no doubt, aware, were you to draw a straight line sixty miles eastward from Philadelphia to the ocean, it would terminate right here. Philly's abominable summers require an escape and we provide the nearest breath of sea breeze, which is to say that it was a can't-miss business proposition. My father was one of the first to see the opportunities. He had a small glass factory only fifteen miles inland. He bought land on Absecon when people thought he was crazy to pay three cents an acre. He invested as a part owner in the very first guest house near the sea. But it was a huge gamble. He died a debtor."

Pace, a man who enjoyed the sound of his voice, seeing that he had my attention, was happy to continue. "My father was there in 1854, waiting, when a train full of newspaper writers was brought in for a complimentary night at my father's hotel. He and his friends had paid for the railroad tickets. The caboose was loaded with ice and food from the finest inns in Philadelphia. It was a grand success. But that was a day when there was a strong ocean breeze that blew the bugs back to the mainland. The newspapermen wrote good stories about the train, the accommodations, and the invigorating salt air. For the next few weeks, the small trains were full. But it didn't last. I fear that many visitors returned to Philadelphia with an altogether different kind of story.

"I will tell you how bad it was. In those early years, we could not even keep horses here; everyone walked everywhere. Horses absolutely could not be controlled. They'd either bolt, sometimes dragging the buggies into the surf. Or they would drop to their knees, still in harness, and try to roll around on their bloodied backs. The greenhead fly draws blood, you know, and rips the flesh as painfully as a hornet sting. That's why we needed the Boardwalks. We couldn't wheel luggage from the station to the hotels through the sand.

"Then came the Civil War, and development really slowed down. We didn't even have a regular train schedule again until the early Seventies. Even so, land speculation continued. Father was wise – he didn't sell any land. In '72, when the regular trains started again, over a thousand rental units and hotel rooms had been built, all with screened windows. Everyone lowered the prices. Still, we weren't doing good business. Speculative money kept coming in, but not enough visitor money. More rooming houses. More hotels. Very little profit. Father passed away in '73."

We pulled up to the second house down from the Boardwalk on Connecticut Avenue. The rental was more than we could afford, more than a hundred a month. It was a big white house with a red, knee-tile roof. On the way back to William and the *Doozey*, Ida whispered to me that she didn't like the kitchen.

"Maybe some place not so fancy," I said.

To be friendly, I tried to catch the chauffeur's eye as we resumed our seats, but he avoided looking at us. Soon enough, I would learn Billy DeWease's reasons for the cold shoulder.

"Take us to the house on Rhode Island Avenue," Pace said.

I asked him to continue the story about the mosquitoes. "Much was at stake," he pronounced. "Even today, we all contribute to the Chamber of Commerce's Insect Eradication Account. Back in the Sixties and Seventies, some of the money went to maintain smoky fires upwind of the hotels and boarding houses. It wasn't a good solution. Our visitors came for healthful ocean breezes, not black smoke. Even with the smoke, people had to seek shelter on the screened porches from the mosquito clouds when the wind was wrong. Sometimes you had to shout to be heard over the sound of them.

"The money goes to taming the marsh. When I was a boy, I loved the marsh. It was a like a lush pasture of salt grass that swayed in stands ten-feet high. There were many bog creatures like muskrats, raccoons, herons and big snakes. I had a narrow, flat bottomed boat that I used to pole through it as a boy. Let me tell you, I never failed to catch large fish there in the winter and early spring, before the mosquitoes and the greenheads hatched.

"The way we got the pestilence under control was to hire crews of niggers and had them set up camp all around the island side and the mainland side of the marsh. Every winter, for years, we had them burning down the marsh. The railroad brought in the barrels of coal oil which the niggers loaded on barges. They started from the edges, pouring it over each little stand of grass and setting it on fire. After awhile, there were clear channels that made it easier for the barges to go from one grassy island to the next. Also, by then, there was so much coal oil floating around that it poisoned a lot of the insects.

"By '75, enough of the marsh was destroyed that it was usually safe, depending on which way the wind blew, for folks to count on not being eaten alive. By the Nineties, ten-car trains were leaving from the terminal in Camden, just across the Delaware River from Philadelphia, every hour. In the summer, they are usually full."

Such people as Mr. Pace talk about "kikes" the same way they talk about "niggers." Even though he was a very interesting person, I started forming a different opinion of the man.

We came to the tip of the island and turned left onto Maine Avenue, a street that ran beside a narrow, raised boardwalk and relatively calm waters .

"This is the Inlet neighborhood," said Mr. Pace. "That's Brigantine Island over there, across the Inlet." He pointed to a low spit of sand with a few houses on it a mile or so across the water. "The tide pours in and out of the Bay through the channel between Brigantine and Absecon Island. This neighborhood is mostly year-round people. It's not fancy, but you might like it. The nigger neighborhood is pretty close, but you don't have to worry, they know their place."

We made another left and drove inland for a couple of blocks, pulling up in front of a three-story house with narrow alleys separating it from its neighbors on either side. We climbed a set of steps to a roofed porch and waited for Pace to unlock the door.

Almost immediately, I knew that Ida liked what she saw, especially the kitchen, the biggest room in the house. I liked the fact that it had a two-bedroom apartment on the ground floor that I could rent out to defray the mortgage.

It had turned warm by late morning. As we stood on the porch of 113 North Rhode Island Avenue, talking about signing the lease, a large truck with its load covered by a tarpaulin came up the street. William, the chauffeur, waved at the men in the front seat. The truck slowed and stopped next to the *Doozey*.

Pace said, "William lives in this neighborhood. His father owns a trawler that ties up just down the street, on a canal leading to the Inlet waters."

Ida said, "Fresh fish would be very nice."

William stepped back from the truck and it continued on its way. I noticed a gap where the rope did not quite pull the canvas together at the back. In the gap, I saw the end of a crate with a braided rope handle and a stenciled blue star. I would have paid it little mind, had William not cast a quick, wary look up to the porch. I averted my eyes and pretended that I had seen nothing out of the ordinary, that I had not recognized the star on the box as a U.S. Army insignia. As I watched the vehicle continue toward the canal, there was no water was dripping from the truck. The day was certainly warm enough to melt ice. What else, I wondered, happened on North Rhode Island Avenue besides fishing?

When we returned to the hotel, the girls were in the lobby talking with two bellhops. Helen waved and came over to meet us in front of the elevators. Pauline, all smiles, ignored us, giving her attention to one of the young men. When she saw Ida approaching, she broke off her conversation, wiggled her fingers at the bellhops, and walked straight past Ida to join me and Helen. The girls were uncharacteristically silent in the elevator. They sensed their mother's anger. Their mother, I knew, didn't want to make a scene in front of the elevator operator.

Ida let loose the moment she closed the door to our suite. "What are you doing talking to those boys? They're working. We're guests here. You know better than to be friendly with servants while they're working. What's the matter with you?"

Pauline said, "Mom, we were just talking. Being friendly is just part of their job, I think." Helen, silent, watched her little sister do the talking.

Ida was having none of it. "Don't talk to me like you're stupid. I know that you know better than to think that boys are just doing their jobs by talking to the likes of you two. Is this what's gonna be if we live in Atlantic City? Because we're not going to do it if you two start acting crazy, if we can't trust you to go out for a stroll on the Boardwalk without getting into trouble."

Both girls looked at the floor. Helen was the darker one, with an olive complexion, like mine, deep brown eyes and long eye lashes. She was a little bit shy, just like a young lady with such a pretty figure ought to be.

Pauline was taller, with her mother's creamy complexion, rosy cheeks, blue eyes and light brown hair. She liked to show off her figure, and she would talk to anyone, except her parents, at the drop of a hat.

"Well?" said Ida.

"Yes, Mama," Helen said.

"Yes," said Pauline. But she didn't look up. Instead, she turned away and went to the window.

We spent the rest of the afternoon telling the girls about the house we'd decided to rent. Soon, the conversation about the bellhops was forgotten as we talked about setting up housekeeping after the school year.

I saw them off on the 5 PM train. I had an appointment with the manager of *Steel Pier* the following day, the famous George Hamid, a person the newspapers call an "impresario." I'd never met one of those before.

Wheel of Fortune

The day of the shooting on the pier, the day I was introduced to the impresario, I met Mike for breakfast in the hotel coffee shop. He had the newspaper open to the sports page.

"Your Ath-u-letics seem a sound bunch, this year," he said as I sat across the table. He was talking about the A's, one of Philadelphia's baseball teams. "Them Yankees, though. Them Yankees may spoil it all for them." We discussed how the sports writers favored the A's to win the American League pennant. Mike scoffed, saying that he wouldn't bet on the pennant until after the Fourth of July.

We left the hotel and walked to the *Steel Pier* on the near-empty Boardwalk, enjoying the morning sunshine. The far end of *Steel Pier* is in the ocean, a quarter of a mile past where the waves break onto the beach. For fifty cents customers buy one ticket that that gets them onto the pier. They buy tickets good for the two theatres, the exhibition spaces, the water circus, both dance halls, the fishing platforms and any of the rides. Food, drink, games on the midway and souvenirs, such as my pictures, were paid with cash.

I was surprised that Mike greeted the ticket taker by name. He said, "Top of the mornin', Seamus."

"Michael," said the man, "Can I have a moment?"

As I waited on the other side of the turnstile, I watched as Mike carried on a whispered conversation with the fellow. Mike was preoccupied after he rejoined me on the other side of the turnstile, as if Seamus had conveyed worrisome news.

He led me up a stairway to a large office space over-looking the beach. A short athletic man with glasses, George Hamid, rose to greet us.

Mike said, "George, take good care of me mate, here. I've got some business with the men. Did Nucky discuss his arrangements with you at all?"

"Don't worry," said Hamid. "Nucky's advised me of all the particulars. All the particulars. Our friend is in good hands. No worrying." I couldn't place George's accent. From the name, I assumed that he was Arabic.

"You're planning to have the place open for Decoration Day, I hear."

"Is May 31st too soon?" I asked. "Can I be ready, do you think."

"Ab... so... lutely!" proclaimed the impresario. "No problem at all. And a good thing, too. Always good to get the season off to a good start. Especially this year."

"This is a special year?"

"Oh, I think so. Absolutely. Much has been invested in the Convention Hall, the grand opening, you know. We expect big crowds, lots of important visitors. Not that we don't usually do something special to open the season, but this should be the biggest opening day of all time. Believe you me — the biggest.

"We always have the veterans going marching down the Boardwalk to open the season. That will be the same. You know, we still have quite a few of the old GAR fellows from the Civil War. Proud men, very proud. And, of course, lots of the younger men from the Great War and the Spanish War and the Philippines War. You know, they're all done up in their nice uniforms and medals. Oh, we have terrific parades. Just terrific! Don't you love the flags and the marching bands with the tubas and the glockenspiels and everything? I do, I do. But, of course, it's in my blood. I used to be in the circus, you know. Center ring, an acrobat."

"But what if it rains?" I asked.

"Don't be silly," replied the impresario. "We'll just have the parades in the Convention Hall! No matter what, this year, it should be the... very... best parade ever in Atlantic City. Nucky didn't mention nothing to you about the Convention Hall?"

You couldn't help noticing the Convention Hall on the way into town. People were usually impressed when they saw the Atlantic City skyline because they'd been driving in the pine forest and tree-lined streets of little New Jersey towns for the whole ride from Philadelphia, so they were not used to seeing so much sky and such a broad horizon. Then, a couple of miles from the shore, they'd make the turn at Pleasantville and see the ultra-modern, brick and concrete towers of Atlantic City standing against all of that sky. That year, 1929, the huge building with a curved roof, the new Convention Hall, had been erected, plain to see from miles away.

"Now that you mention it, he did talk about it," I lied, hoping to quell the man's enthusiasm; I felt under assault. I capped my pen and slid the rental agreement across the desk. He looked over my signatures. Then he signed using the pen, the ink and the blotter from a bronze desk set. He handed me one copy, put the other into a folder, and offered me a cigar from a humidor that matched the desk set. We lit up; I blew a beautiful, fat ring that floated toward a window overlooking the beach. The deal was done.

"Nucky is very proud of the Convention Hall. As a member of the Convention Bureau Board of Directors, I have myself personally visited the construction site on many, many occasions. Let me tell you, Mr. Rubin, it is amazing in there. You would be amazed. Did you know that it is… the… largest… auditorium… in the whole wide world?" he asks. "Seven acres under a single roof without one pillar, without one post or one column to obstruct a person's view. Did Nucky happen to mention that?"

I shrugged.

"Well," Hamid continued, "We're gonna dedicate the place on Decoration Day. We have invited all the big shots, and they're almost all coming. We got your Senators, we got your Governors, we got your Congressmen, and your Mayors." And, I thought to myself, one special Director.

Hamid had not let up, "We're giving them all complimentary hotel reservations. That's how Nucky does things; he gives away complimentary this and that – big stuff, little stuff. The big shots will sit in the reviewing stand above the Boardwalk with a view of the ocean. That was one of the things I, personally, insisted about. I insisted. 'We have to have a nice reviewing stand,' I said. Everybody liked my idea. So we got them to build the end of the Convention Hall that's on the Boardwalk as a reviewing stand. It's got Roman columns holding up a roof that's long enough to fly a hundred flags. At least a hundred." He blew a smoke ring, as good as mine. "We're having a Grand Army of the Republic Decoration Day Dedication Ball, the very first official event to be held in the… very… largest… the… most modern… auditorium in the whole wide world. You'll come."

He opened a desk drawer and took out a note pad. "I got your name and address on the lease. How many people you want to bring to the Ball?" he asked. "I'll see you get the engraved invitations Special Delivery."

What should I have said? That I couldn't come because I'd be waiting inside a secret room to take secret pictures of one of his big shots? I told him four tickets for Mr. and Mrs. Albert Rubin and Family. I assumed that Ida, who loved to dance, would like to go. Maybe Mike or Sam would dance with her as I did my job at *The Ritz*, The girls, of course, love to dress up in their gowns, the ones they wear to weddings and Bar Mitzvahs.

Hamid told me where to find the maintenance chief so I could see my location and talk about the arrangements. So I said goodbye to the impresario, and went back downstairs.

The exhibition hall was closed to the public while they were putting up a new show for the summer. There was a lot of construction and I had to watch my step. I saw a freshly painted sign, "Treasures of the Pharaohs." I guessed that the new exhibit was going to be the... world's... most... something.

The engineer, his name was DiFranco, was waiting for me. He saw me come down from the offices and introduced himself. We left the exhibition space and went out into the midway, the wooden street that runs the whole length of the pier.

The theatres and dance halls lined both sides of the midway. During high season, men sat on stools outside the theatres, in charge of the velvet ropes. A billboard announced that Red Skelton, the famous comedian from the radio, would be performing during the Decoration day weekend.

Everything was wood construction. "Mr. DiFranco, why do they call it the *steel* pier?"

"I'm Ant'ony," he said. "Call me Tony. The underneath is steel girders and deep, deep steel pilings in cement way down into the sand. Very strong. Nothing moves here, even in big waves. I got a crew all the time underneath, painting for the rust."

"Call me Al," I said.

I had decided to call my place, *Steel Pier Memories,* imagining a tiny stall in a remote corner, probably near a toilet. Instead, because of Nucky's pull, I had been given a prime spot, exactly in the middle of the pier. The theatres and restaurants were at the covered front half under a single roof. *Memories* was to be just past all of that, but still under the roof.

The location was so much better than I had hoped for. People going for a stroll in the moonlight after leaving the dance hall would pass *Memories*. People on the way back from the water circus at the end of the pier would pass in front of *Memories*. People who'd caught a trophy fish off the pier would come to *Memories*. People still smiling from the vaudeville would want souvenir photographs from *Steel Pier Memories*. Who would be able to resist having a personalized souvenir at such a location? Who?

The space was also bigger than I had expected. I saw that it could accommodate a darkroom. Tony assured me that the water piped in from the mainland is pure and reliable and that I could have as many electrical outlets as I needed for studio lights and printers. "Whatever you want," said Tony. I sketched a layout on graph paper that he had on his clipboard. Over the course of an hour we made lots of changes until we both thought we had a good floor plan.

The last thing we decided was the sign. We walked around, looking at the different styles. Above a popcorn stall, I saw a sign with modern lettering that didn't have any of the old-fashioned curlicues. I liked it. I decided that *Steel Pier Memories* should be painted with blue letters on a white background with a simple, red filigree border around the edges of the sign, like the gilt stamped onto the covers of my most expensive leather-bound albums. The sign would be surrounded with light bulbs like a theatre marquee.

Tony's sign painter was Paolo a master craftsman, just over from Italy. We found him at work on a sandwich board that was to go out front, on the Boardwalk. The sign was almost finished. "New! Under Sea Aquarium! Wonders of the Deep!" Paolo spoke no English, but listened carefully to Tony, nodding his head, saying, "Si, si."

I used a sheet of the graph paper to draw the filigree border as I remembered it.

"How about the scenery with the holes cut out? Can your painter make those for me?"

I made three sketches of what I wanted and gave the crude drawings to Paolo. In one of them, a man and a woman in bathing costumes stand on the beach with the Atlantic City skyline behind them. In the same lettering as the sign, it says, "Atlantic City Queen of Resorts." The other sketch featured the body of a child straddling a dolphin rising from the waves under the lettering, "Atlantic City by The Sea." On the third sketch, a sexy lady in a bathing suit wears a sash that says "Miss America."

Tony and I talked about a schedule and he said that he'd be ready to set up my equipment next weekend; seeing as I was a friend of Mike's, he'd get everyone started right away. We shook hands, and I went off in search of Mike.

It was around noon and, even though it was a weekday in the middle of May, there was already some trade walking along the midway. I spotted Mike standing with Seamus, the man who had been collecting tickets at the entrance to the pier. They were at one of the gaming booths, a Wheel of Fortune, talking with the barker who spun the wheel. Kewpie dolls and carnival glass *tchatchkes* lined a shelf. As I approached, I could see that the Wheel of Fortune operator was scowling.

Suddenly, Seamus, the ticket taker, reached across the counter, grabbed the operator by his shirt front and pulled him halfway across the counter with numbers in little boxes painted on it for people to place their one cent bets.

73

Seamus was nose-to-nose with the man and said, "You'll pay it back, you sorry sod."

Mike saw me and said, "Al, why don't ye wait for me down at the entrance?"

I was about to say that there was no need, that my business there was finished, that I'd find my way back, get my car, and return to Philadelphia. But my presence was enough of a distraction that Seamus lost his concentration, and the Wheel of Fortune operator pulled free, lurched backward, hitting the shelf with a thump that sent most of the Kewpie dolls tumbling down.

Seamus started to climb over the counter. The operator reached into his pants pocket and pulled out a little pistol. Mike, Seamus and I jumped back, holding our hands in front of us. We continued backing away until we were almost on the opposite side of the midway.

I saw flame spit from the barrel, heard the crack of two shots, and watched Seamus stagger backwards to fall against the shuttered front of a shop. Mike started toward the operator, then looked down to see Seamus's bloody chest and shoulder. Mike knelt next to him. The operator saw his opportunity, flipped up a portion of the counter, darted through the opening into the midway, and sprinted toward the entrance of the Pier.

Seamus put a hand to his shoulder. He lifted it and saw it drenched in his blood. "Mother of God," he said. "The thievin' bastard shot me. Mother of God. Mother of God. Mother of God, Mother of God, forgive me all me sins and me trespasses. Oh, Mother of God. Oh the son of a bitch." His eyes rolled up and he went still.

Mike put his fingers to Seamus neck, feeling for a pulse. Then he put his ear to the man's mouth, listening for breath sounds. He stood, and I realized that a small crowd had gathered around. Mike hollered, "This man needs a doctor. Is there a doctor here?"

A man came and knelt next to Seamus. Mike grabbed my upper arm. He said, "Quick. Come away."

I felt that I must stay, to help the man bleeding so profusely onto the boards of the midway. Mike tugged harder, almost pulling me off my feet. "He ain't dead. I think he'll be okay. Quick," he repeated. "Come away."

We walked against a tide of people who were attracted by the sound of gunshots and the commotion behind us. When we emerged through the turnstiles onto The Boardwalk in front of the pier, Mike crossed to the ramp that led down to the sidewalk of Virginia Avenue. I followed, dazed, as he strolled along the pavement as if nothing had happened. I looked down at my hands and saw that they were shaking. Around me, sounds were muffled and colors washed out. Michael looked at me and said, "Keep up now, Al. We don't want to be attracting attention."

"Aha," I said, as if comprehending a profound, new idea.

We came to the corner of Virginia and Pacific Avenues, a long block from the pier. A jitney was approaching us, heading uptown. Its top was down, most of its seats empty. I heard distant sirens. Mike said, "If anyone asks about me, tell them I've set sail. Not to worry. I'll handle it."

"Tell who? Set sail? Michael, what's happening?" I was dumbfounded, watching Mike board the jitney.

He reached into his pocket and handed the driver his nickel. He turned toward me as the long touring car pulled away from the curb.

"You know who. The bosses."

Federal Agents

I took the jitney in the opposite direction, downtown, and got off at Iowa Avenue. I walked across the inlaid marble of the *Ritz Carlton* lobby and knocked on Lou Kessel's office door. When I got no answer, I asked a desk clerk to call Nucky's apartment and ask for Lou. He looked at me skeptically, his way of letting me know that I wasn't the sort of person normally allowed an audience with the Czar of the Ritz. He cocked an eyebrow at the response he got. "Go right up," he said with considerably more respect. "Ninth floor."

That was another moment when I ought to have walked away from the edge. But I was so fully in the throes of seduction that even if *Hashem*, Reb Mendel's name for God, had warned me of the impending disaster by telegram, I would probably have ignored it. I was trivializing gunshots and bloody wounds as if they were normal business.

Looking back, I see that it wasn't just the greed working on me, it was snobbery. I felt inflated by the way the clerk changed his attitude when he understood that I would be welcomed by the Czar. Nucky's status, Sam's style, Mike's authority on the pier, even Hamid's deference to me as a friend of Nucky's — all these were as seductive as the prospect of earning big money on the *Steel Pier*.

A Negro maid was waiting for me as I left the elevator. She opened Nucky's elaborately carved wooden door, the kind with polished brass hinges and etched glass panels that you'd see on a mansion. She escorted me through a large foyer and into a parlor and offered me a seat on one of the upholstered sofas.

There was twice as much furniture as I had seen in Sam's penthouse. In Nucky's place, the paintings on the walls were oil portraits of men with side whiskers and ladies wearing gowns and big necklaces. Two sets of floor-to-ceiling French doors opened to a broad terrace. I told the maid that I'd wait out there.

I was smoking a cigarette, inspecting the horizon, when Lou came rolling out. "What happens?" he demanded. "Crazy George Hamid calls me. He says Irish are shooting on his Pier. You came with Mike Finnerty. He says you disappear. Mike Finnerty disappears. He can't find neither one of you. What happens? Tell me."

I explained what I'd witnessed, "All of a sudden, this Wheel of Fortune man pulls out a gun and starts shooting at Michael and this other fellow, who was the ticket collector at the entrance to the Pier. That's the man who got shot, the ticket collector."

"Michael and his hooligans! I just knew it! Crazy Irish! Tell me whole story."

I explained how I arrived just at the moment the gun came out and described the gory details. When I was finished, Lou asked me, "And Finnerty? Where's he at now?"

"He took a jitney and said that you and Nucky should know that he's set sail, that everything is going to be okay, that Michael will handle it."

"Which way? The jitney?"

"Uptown," I said.

Lou asked me to stay for awhile. He said to Linda, the maid, to bring me whatever I wanted to drink. I asked if she might bring me a sandwich instead. I was chewing on a peanut butter and jelly when Nucky joined me on the terrace. He was wearing a silk robe over silk pajamas and leather slippers and holding a tall glass of orange juice.

"Albert," he said. "So good to see you. I understand you've had a rather distressing day."

"Hello, Nucky," I replied. "It was horrible. Just horrible. But, it wasn't all bad. I'm all set up with Mr. George Hamid, thanks to you. I got a terrific location on the Pier, maybe the best, again thanks to you. I met with the maintenance chief, too. A terrific guy, and he knows exactly what I need. So the shooting wasn't the only thing."

"Very good. Good for you. I'm happy George was able to help you out. Listen, Albert, the police should talk to you. You shouldn't have run off like that."

"I'm sorry, Nucky. I don't know what came over me. Mike wouldn't let me stay. He just about pulled me off the pier. Then he took off uptown. I came right back here. Is Sam in town today? Should I call him?"

"I'll have Lou talk to Sam. You should try not to involve yourself," he said, downing the entire glass of juice with a couple of swallows. "I'm going to ask the chief of detectives to take a statement from you. Will that be alright?"

"Absolutely," I said.

"I'll call him now. It shouldn't take long."

"You mean here? He'll come here?"

"You'd rather go to the police station?" asked the Czar. "There's no need. Why don't you meet him in your suite downstairs? I know Lieutenant Howarth very well. I'm sure he won't mind."

Twenty minutes later I was in the armchair in the fifth floor suite answering questions from two policemen in plain clothes. They sat side-by-side on the couch; Lieutenant Howarth asked the questions, Detective Canterbury took the notes. Lou Kessel sat in the chair next to mine. Somehow, he gave the impression that he was in charge.

Canterbury took out his notebook, fountain pen poised. Howarth asked me if I knew the man who got shot or the Wheel of Fortune man. "Just Mike. He's the one I know. I don't know anything about the other two. I had just come up to them when they started fighting and the shooting happened. All in a second. I don't remember much. Is the man who got shot all right?"

"We don't know. They took him to the hospital. Finnerty knows them both? The shooter and the victim?" asked Howarth.

"Apparently."

"What was your business on the pier?"

So then I had to explain that I've known Michael for a long time. It occurred to me that they might think that I was talking too much, so I decided to shut up. Soon, the detectives realized that I'd told them everything I was going to, and they got up from the sofa. Before they left, they took my phone number and address in Philadelphia and the name of my new business, *Steel Pier Memories*. I had the distinct impression that they had no real interest in me – I was just a witness, an innocent bystander.

I had to get back to Philadelphia, to Ida and our studio. I packed up and checked out. I crossed Pacific Avenue to my parked *De Soto*, whistling the only circus tune I knew. The song stayed in my head for the whole drive across South Jersey, as did an image of the impresario taking triumphant bows in a spotlight, "His moves they are gracefullll, the girls he does pleeease, that daring young man on the flying trapeeeze."

I came over the bridge from Camden and saw the Delaware River far, far below. There I was, driving my own automobile over the longest suspension bridge in the world. What a city! What a country! Compared to the life my father had led, I was living like a prince. My father hadn't even had a horse, whereas I had a 1929 *De Soto*!

He'd had a pushcart with sewing supplies. I had a photography studio. Seven of us had lived in three tiny rooms in a *shtetl*. I owned a three story building with a garden in the back.

I took Market Street into West Philadelphia. The shade trees were stippled with springtime green and the lawn azaleas were glowing in the late daylight. It was after six by the time I parked the car. Ida had closed the studio. I found her in the kitchen.

All the way home in the De Soto, I debated with myself about whether I would tell her about the shooting. I don't lie to my wife, but sometimes I leave things out. For example, I hadn't told her that I almost saw her cousin slap a woman in the face. Why should she have known about the shooting on the pier? We had no part in Sam's business or Mike's business. Our business was taking pictures.

Instead of standing there with her hands on her hips and giving me what-for, which was what I had been expecting, she came over for a hug. Nice.

"Al, you're so late. All I could think of was your car smashed into a tree. You should call if you're going to be late."

Helen, the older one, came into the kitchen to help Ida get the table ready for supper. "We were worried about you," she said.

"Nothing to worry about. Just business."

Pauline came in as Ida was putting the lamb chops on the table. I told them all about *Steel Pier*. "*Memories* is going to be very good, I think. They have a sign painter, who's really an artist, who is going to paint me these beautiful paintings of the beach and the sea with holes cut out for the customers to stick their faces into. They have me set up right in the middle of the pier. It's under the roof but open to the midway. And guess what? I'll need a person out front to take care of the trade while I'm taking the pictures. It's very important. You'll work."

Neither daughter volunteered. Instead, Pauline said, "Pass the potatoes, please."

I waited awhile longer. "Really. I will need a person, maybe all three of you, with me all the time. There's no school. You'll have to work, both of you." Still, I waited to hear enthusiastic exclamations of how they want to work with their Papa.

"You'll work," said Ida.

Then I told them about Hamid, what an interesting fellow he was. "We may be getting invited to the big Ball. They are opening that new convention hall on Decoration Day. The night before, all the big shots are having a Ball. The boss of the pier is sending us, all of us, an invitation."

The rest of the evening was taken up with a discussion of what to wear to the ball.

The next morning, two men wearing dark suits and dark hats came through the shop door as I was alone in the studio, sorting through last afternoon's delivery from Hermann's lab. The trolley sounds from Chester Avenue came in with them.

"Mr. Albert Rubin?"

"And what can I do for you?"

"Would you mind giving us a bit of your time," said one of them. "About Monday. About the shooting you witnessed."

"And who exactly are you?"

"We are agents of the United States Government." One of them removed a sheet of folded paper from his jacket pocket and handed it to me. Opened up, it said that Oscar Whitehead was an authorized agent of the Investigations Bureau of the United States Department of Justice. The other one handed me a similar piece of paper. His name was Eleazer Dixon. These were Hoover's men.

"Delighted to make your acquaintance."

Then the customers started to come in. Whitehead and Dixon said they'd wait outside until we could talk. As I shooed the third customer out the door, twisted the sign around and pulled down the shade. "We can talk now." I said, inviting the men on the sidewalk to come in.

"It was a terrible business," I said. "Just terrible. Have they caught that man with the gun? The Wheel of Fortune man?"

Instead of answering, the one named Dixon asked, "Where were you born, Mr. Rubin?"

"I was born in a village outside of the city of Ungvar, way at the eastern end of Hungary. The province of Ruthenia."

"So," said Dixon, "Hungary."

"That depends on who you ask. When the War was finished, they took it away from Austria-Hungary, because there was no more Austria-Hungary, and they made it part of that new country, Czechoslovakia. But the village where I grew up is right on the border where Czechoslovakia, Romania and the Ukraine, which is part of the Soviet Union now, which also wasn't there before, where they all meet. There's a little bit of country that they couldn't agree on called The Ruthenian Free State, which is actually where I came from. So you could say any one of those. Except Hungary. They definitely took it away from Hungary."

Agent Whitehead was blinking. Agent Dixon said, "If you were to go home and visit family, what country would you get your visa from?"

"First, I don't have any family left there. My brothers are here and in Baltimore. I have cousins who live in Vienna, and another bunch of cousins in Budapest. But I can't say anymore which country I was born in."

Agent Whitehead finally said something, "What language did you speak?"

"Hungarian. We learned to read and write Hungarian in the school. A little Russian. And we knew German because it's like Yiddish, which is what we used with family and so forth. And Hebrew for the temple. Why do you want to know what language I spoke? I speak English. Why do you want to know where I was born? I'm an American citizen. I have been one since as soon as I could be one, seven years after I got here. In 1912 I took the test. I did the pledge of allegiance. Do you want to hear me say it?"

"That won't be necessary," said Dixon. "Since you speak Hungarian, we'll put down Hungary, okay?"

"Put down where? In what file is this going? May I ask, why do you have to put down where I came from?"

"It's just for our records," said Whitehead.

I stared at them, remembering what Sam had said about Hoover deporting people. Can they deport citizens? "Sure, sure," I said. "Put down Hungary."

All of a sudden, Dixon asked, "Who is Mr. Michael Finnerty?"

"Michael Finnerty is our friend. He's my friend. He used to live around the corner. See this wall behind me? Mike and I built it together."

"How long ago was this?"

They were very interested in "Mr. Finnerty," asking the same questions different ways, taking notes. I told them I was happy to see that he had found a steady job working at my wife's cousin's restaurant, *Babette's*. I told them that he was the one who introduced me to the business manager of the *Steel Pier*, Mr. George Hamid.

Customers came to the door, saw the sign, and walked away. Then Whitehead said, "So you know Mr. Sam Brodsky, also?"

"Since he was a little boy. I told you, he's my wife's cousin."

"Have you seen him lately?"

"Sure. With Mr. Nucky Johnson. We had a nice dinner at Sam's restaurant. It was business, really. I'm going to have a photo studio on *Steel Pier*. Mr. Johnson helped make the arrangements."

They asked a lot of questions about Sam. I didn't talk about the visit to the casino.

When I tried to talk about the shooting, Whitehead said something that frightened me, "We have all that information from your report to the Atlantic City Police. The shooting is their business, not ours."

Nu? I asked myself. What kind of Justice Department investigators are not interested in a crime like firing a gun on a pier crowded with people just out to have a good time? What *were* they interested in?

Finally, I was happy to see them close their notebooks. But they didn't leave. Dixon handed me a business card and said, "You must call us if you need to. In fact, why don't you just give us a call next week, just to let us know how things are going? Is Wednesday morning good for you?"

I looked at Eleazer Dixon's card. It said he was a "special" agent. "No, I don't think Wednesday is good for me."

"What day is good for you?"

"I'll call you," I said.

Dixon's eyes narrowed. Whitehead, hands at his sides, stood waiting.

"I'd really like it if I know when I'll hear from you," said Dixon,

"Gentlemen, I appreciate your position. Please consider mine. I'm going to be busy the next several weeks. I told you that I will be setting up a business on the *Steel Pier* and it must be done before Decoration Day. Really, a lot to do. I will keep your card and gladly call you when business is not so pressing. Please?"

Dixon thought it over and softened a little. Finally, Whitehead said, "We'll look for you on the Pier, then?"

It was getting worse – they would make a special trip to Atlantic City just to talk to me. "Absolutely," I said. "When can I expect you?"

"How's Wednesday morning sound?"

"I'll probably be there. If not, ask Mr. Hamid or Mr. DiFranco." As they were on their way out, I twisted the sign and reopened Albert's Photography. "So long. It was a pleasure to make your acquaintance."

As I ushered a waiting customer inside, I heard Dixon call over his shoulder, "Wednesday."

Gabriel

We must have gotten a hundred phone calls from people who saw our ad. We'd placed it in four newspapers. It said we were looking for summer help, for a person who understood photography, who could be an assistant. So why did we get ninety calls from people who didn't know a lens from *latke*? We had made appointments to conduct interviews with a whole bunch of them who sounded like possibilities. But then we decided to hire Gabriel Golden after the first morning of interviews. Next time, I told myself, if I ever needed to hire a person, I would use an employment agency. We had to call all the other people and apologize and tell them not to bother coming to Albert Photos for a job interview.

Ida and I had been taking turns at the counter while the other one was interviewing in the studio. Then we'd switch so that we both had a chance to talk to the person.

Gabe Golden showed up a little early, and I kept an eye on him while he waited his turn. He examined the portraits, and then he handled a couple of the sample albums, and finally he started reading the price list that he picked up from the end of the counter. He went back to the portraits, getting up very close to peer at details. His shoes were polished and his collar was clean.

When it was Gabriel's turn, because I recognized his accent and because he said he saw the ad in the *Jewish Exponent,* I knew that he was a greenhorn. In Yiddish, we established the fact that he was from near Kiev in the Ukraine and that I am from near Ungvar in Godknowswhere. Then, I made a point of going back to English.

I came around the counter and went to the portrait of the lady with the pearls. "Tell me about this picture," I said.

"Something about the lighting. There are shadows, but very soft. And the focus is very fine, a small depth of field." His English was excellent.

"So. Very good *boychik.* How come you know so much about photography? Such a young fellow."

"I was in the Photography Club for all four years. In Germany. At the Gymnasium. In Hamburg."

Many Jewish families were living in port cities like Hamburg while they waited for visas to the United States. If they couldn't get the right paperwork, or if something happened to the relative who was sponsoring them, maybe they would have to stay in those cities forever. It was not as easy as it had been in years past, before The Great War. It seemed that Americans were getting tired of so many immigrants. The Congress kept tightening the rules, making it more and more difficult for people to qualify for a visa, lowering the quotas for people from Central and Eastern European countries. So, four years was not so long those days. Ida had sisters with families in Ruthenian Free State. She had been begging them to come to Philadelphia, but they didn't want to leave.

"A little's not good enough. Did you develop pictures? Did you work in the darkroom?"

"Yes, quite a bit."

"Okay," I said. "Come with me. Show me what you learned at the Gymnasium. In Hamburg, no less." Not everybody goes to a gymnasium, which is an academic high school. I ushered him through the studio door and said, "Okay, *boychik*. Tell me what you see."

I'd painted the wall behind the sitter's chair with merging cloud shapes in tones of green, blue, and red. The other three walls were stark white. The studio camera sat on a heavyweight tripod.

Gabe said, "The camera has a regular 4 inch by 5 inch back plane. You're still using glass plate. This bellows can extend very far. More than a meter. Very long. This is how you get such fine focusing." He looked around at the equipment. He said, "To manage shadows, you use a white umbrella, some mirrors on stands, a spotlight, and a theater foot light. You put different colored filters on the foot light to change the tone of the background and the hues of the skin."

I asked him to tell me about the camera. He studied the engraving on the black lens ring. "This looks like a nice, compound lens, but I never heard of the maker." I was not surprised; it was an English lens and too expensive to show up at a student camera club. But I was impressed that he understood the optics.

"How come you have the summer off? Are you a student."

"Yes," he said. "I am at the University of Pennsylvania; I have just finished my first year."

Penn, I'd been told, was the best college in the city. Only the rich could go there. So why did somebody rich enough to go to Penn need a summer job?

"They gave me a scholarship," he said.

Until then, I thought that the only Jews that they let into Penn were from the old German-Jewish families like the Solis-Cohens or the Gratzes, families who had been in Philadelphia since grown men wore knee pants, when Pennsylvania was still a colony. That they would have given a greenhorn from Kiev a scholarship, which is a very fine thing, was something I had not known.

"And your family? Your mother and father?"

"My father works for my uncle Sol, in the dry goods business. Wholesale. On South Street."

"So, you can't work for your Uncle Sol?"

Gabriel Golden smiled. "Cameras are nicer," he said. He asked about the pay and the hours. Then he wanted to know if there might be any darkroom work and could he use the darkroom for his own photographs. We went into the darkroom where I had some prints from the experimental film hanging to dry. I could tell he wanted to try out my enlarger.

"We'll see," I said. "Maybe after hours, if you pay for your supplies."

There came a knock on the darkroom door and Helen, who knew it was okay to come in if the red light was not on, opened the door and said, "Pop, Mom went up. She said for you to be upstairs at 6 o'clock."

"Okay, Okay."

"You always say that."

Gabe turned to see who was talking. Helen seemed a bit startled by him. That was when it occurred to me that having such a one as Gabriel around, a single young man, a nice Jewish boy, could create some situations.

"Okay, Okay. I promise. 6 o'clock. Watch the store. I'll be out soon, and we'll close up together." She closed the door.

"When can you start?" I asked him.

"Tomorrow," he said.

"Listen, I have to talk to Mrs. Rubin. Do you have a telephone at your house? Call me tonight." We returned to the storefront where Helen pretended that she didn't notice him. I saw him looking at her.

93

Yentas

The house on Rhode Island Avenue had been vacant during the month of May, so we had been able to move in by stages. In the mornings, before I left Philadelphia, I'd stuff the *De Soto* with boxes of housewares and summer clothes and drive the sixty miles to Rhode Island Avenue. I must have schlepped two dozen cardboard boxes down the narrow back stairs of our Chester Avenue apartment and then up the stairs of the shore house. I left most them unopened for Ida and the girls to unpack when we moved in.

Then I'd lock up the house and go to the pier to work on the lighting, the supplies, and the new equipment. I didn't worry about Chester Avenue − the studio was in Ida and Gabriel's competent hands. Every night, after working to set up the studio on *Steel Pier*, I drove back to Philadelphia, often arriving after Ida and the girls were asleep.

We moved into the house on North Rhode Island Avenue on the weekend before Decoration Day. Our first meal as a family was a roasted a chicken that Ida had shopped for in Philadelphia. My wife surprised us by lighting the *Shabbas* candles and saying the prayers. "For luck in the new house," she said.

It was nice, not because I cared about *Shabbas*, nor did Ida, she hadn't lit the candles in years, but because Ida was still coming up with surprises even after twenty years of marriage.

We were not the kind of people who were strict about religion; we didn't even belong to a synagogue. I guess we were what they call "reformed" Jews. But there was not a Reformed congregation anywhere in our neighborhood. There was a Conservative synagogue, but I had not cared for the rabbi. He tried to make people feel guilty about whether they were being observant enough for his tastes. Who needed that? So we stopped belonging. We bought tickets for the high holy day services: Yom Kippur and Rosh Hashanah. But that was only because Ida insisted that we stay in touch with the Jewish community. She just wanted people to see our faces in the *shul*. Personally, I would rather have bought tickets for a vaudeville or a picture show.

That Saturday morning, six days before Decoration Day, we all went up to Hamid's office where a nice lady named Mariam filled out identification forms and gave each of us a card to show at the entrance. "You can come and go as you please," she said.

"We can get onto the pier for free whenever we want?" Pauline asked.

"Certainly. You work here now," Mariam said.

Decoration Day occurred on a Thursday in 1929, and everyone in Atlantic City expected big crowds through

the weekend. Along the length of the pier, I introduced
my family to people who were painting, stocking and
cleaning their stalls. Across the midway from *Memories*,
an elderly couple were putting all kinds of *chazzerai* on
the display racks of their souvenir shop: ashtrays, beach
towels, post cards, and shot glasses with little paintings of
almost naked ladies. A Polish family named Krucziewsky
had the hot dog stand next door to *Memories*. They were
good people, the kind who kept asking us how we were
doing and did we need any help.

My idea was that all five of us, including Gabriel,
should know how to do everything. That Saturday, even
though it wasn't officially the summer season, there were
people looking for ways to spend their money on the
Steel Pier by ten o'clock in the morning. They saw Paolo's lovely sign in the bright sun, they looked inside and
saw his beach paintings, and they wanted us to take their
pictures. It pained me that we were not yet ready, that we
had to turn them away. There was work to be done and
jobs to be learned.

After I showed Ida, Pauline and Helen what was what,
we started taking pictures of ourselves with our heads in
the holes. We borrowed two of the Kruciewsky kids and
took their pictures sitting on a retired carrousel pony that
I'd repainted.

My three women and Mrs. Kruciewsky each posed
with their heads in the Miss America painting. I planned
to develop and print the exposures that evening so that we

could have them out on display when we opened for business. I still have those pictures somewhere.

"Well, would you look who's here!" Ida exclaimed. I turned from the panel of light switches where I was practicing with the girls and saw Sam Brodsky standing at the entrance to *Memories* with a pretty young lady. I was glad to see him. I had left messages for him with Louie Kessel. I'd sent him a telegram saying that we needed to talk.

He introduced us to his fiancée, Anne Adler. The girls and Ida seemed happy to be distracted. I was too serious about business, Ida always said, and that was why the girls never got excited about helping out. Sue me! They didn't have to be excited, was my attitude, they just had to do their jobs.

The female Rubins inspected the enormous diamond ring Anne was wearing; they gasped in appreciation; they inquired about the wedding plans for next month; they started the process of discovering people they knew in common. "Are you from the Long Island Adlers? Do you know Irv Adler?" And so on. When Ida met someone new, she didn't quit until she had found some kind of connection.

Sam interrupted, "Ida," he said, "Do you mind if I borrow Al for an hour or so? We have some business, if that's okay. Al, shall we have a little stroll? You can teach me about this famous pier." The women seemed pleased to see us go.

J. Edgar Hoover

We walked toward the end of the pier, away from the Boardwalk. I said, "Listen, Sam, I had a visit last week from these two men, Whitehead and Dixon, from the same part of the government as Hoover, the Justice Department. They were special agents in the Investigations Bureau."

"Okay," he said.

"So what does that mean? Shouldn't we stop this business? Do you think maybe they know what we're trying to do."

"*Nah*, not unless you told them."

"Told them? Sam, get serious. But you don't think it's a coincidence? Men from the same department as Hoover coming to my studio?"

"Not exactly a coincidence. I think they are interested in you because of the shooting, your connection to Mike Finnerty."

"Michael? He's mixed up in the IRA, isn't he," I said, voicing my long-held suspicion.

Sam, not one to tell secrets, shook his head. "You'll have to ask Michael," he said.

"Sam, do you know where Michael is? Is he okay?"

"I know exactly where he is, and he is perfectly fine. We're in touch. He'll be around again soon, as soon as the commotion about that stupid shooting on the pier dies down."

"What was the shooting about? How is that man who got shot? Seamus is his name. What about him?"

"Seamus is going to be fine. He caught a small caliber bullet in the shoulder, that's all. He'll be fine."

"So why did Michael run away?"

"The less you know, the better off you are," Sam said.

We watched the waves roll past us toward the beach.

"Sam, I don't know enough about this situation. You know you can count on me to do the job; it's all set up. But please, I am not comfortable being so much in the dark."

"Get over it," he said.

"That's not my way, Sam. There's more to this than you're telling me, and I want to know."

The sun was getting stronger. Sam stood, removed his jacket and draped it over the back of the bench. He faced me, leaned against the railing and crossed his arms. He looked at his watch. "I've got the time. Are you in a hurry?"

"Please, Sam, I'm all ears."

"This guy, this Hoover, he's not your usual guy. I actually saw him once, and ever since, because he made such an impression on me, I've been interested whenever

I see his name in the paper, which is more and more as time goes on.

"I was doing a little business near Herald Square. This was in 1919, I guess I was nineteen. I used to have a craps game that I ran in an alley off the Square for guys to play at lunchtime. So, this one day, we're shooting craps, and I'm holding the stakes, and I'm watching out for trouble like usual, you know how it is. I look out to the end of the alley and I see this crowd starting, which is probably not a good thing for the game. So I stop the play and walk out to the Square to see what's going on.

"There was this little platform going up and a sign that says Emma Goldman is going to speak. I decide to stick around, since I'd heard all kinds of different stories about Emma Goldman and I was curious. You know, some people think she's terrific for organizing women, and for birth control, and for protesting the draft and the Great War, and for standing for the unions against the bosses. And there are other people who hate her for exactly the same things. I think she's in Russia now, one them that got deported. But back then, she was always in the papers.

"Soon, she gets up on the platform. There's maybe a couple dozen people standing around, not a real big crowd. Some men are standing next to the platform holding signs. 'Repeal the Sedition Act,' and 'Worker Justice' and like that. One guy hands me a pamphlet. When Emma Goldman starts to talk, I realize that she is a very good speaker. Not a pretty woman, mind you. But with a very strong voice, the kind you listen to. She starts out saying that she's just out after two years in jail for saying that the draft was illegal and unfair to workers and all that, and that it was unconstitutional.

"But she was really mad about the Sedition Act. She said it was passed so that the Government could arrest people who disagreed with them. Very, very unconstitutional she said.

"That's about as far as she got in her speech because, all of a sudden, from every single side street, all at the same time, a whole lot of paddy wagons pull into the Square. Before you know it, cops are jumping out of the wagons and rushing to the platform, waving their billy clubs. Naturally, I decide to back away.

"But the cops aren't interested in anybody but the guys with the signs and the pamphlets. In a flash, they're dragging them into the paddy wagons, whacking them as they go. Then they're on the platform and leading Emma Goldman down the steps.

"I'm at the corner of 31st Street and Sixth Avenue, backing away, when I notice an official-looking guy who is standing next to a big automobile, holding an open notebook and a fountain pen. That night, in the *New York Times*, I read his name for the first time, J. Edgar Hoover.

"To make a long story short, all the people that got put in the paddy wagons, and a couple hundred more, got put on a boat to Russia. No trial. As far as I was ever able to tell, it was all on Hoover's say-so. The only one of them who ever so much as gave a speech was Emma Goldman, and she was one who did everything out in the open.

"So, for the next couple of months, I watched the papers and, sure enough, Hoover's name kept popping up. It seems that the job he had with the Justice Department was to find out which people are the ones who are trying to overthrow the government. He was in charge of keeping track of them. Even then, he was a big hero in Washington."

I remembered most of what Sam was telling me. Whenever a Jewish person's name gets put in the paper, we take special notice. It's only natural. Emma Goldman had been a powerful woman who made a lot of people nervous. Many Jewish Americans would have preferred for Emma Goldman to shut up and go away – *gey avek*.

My opinion was that she had a right to her opinions and she ought be allowed to speak *because* she was so articulate about what was wrong with the Federal Government. The Government always needs changing; that's why we have politics; that's why we have democracy.

"The thing about Hoover," Sam said, "Is that he takes all of this personally. He really believes he's on a holy mission. What's scary is how much power he has. It's nuts! He's a law unto himself. And then he gets himself made as the *permanent* director of Federal investigations.

That means that even if we get a new President and new Attorney General, he keeps his job. Not a good guy to have on your bad side."

Sam offered me a cigarette from a beautiful silver case. About a quarter mile away, on the *Steeplechase Pier*, I saw workmen on scaffolding. They were putting thousands of light bulbs into what was being touted as the biggest, brightest electrified sign in the world. The *Chesterfield* cigarette company was preparing to turn it on the night before Decoration Day as part of the celebration for the new Convention Hall.

"Sam," I said, "I had no idea you paid so much attention to politics."

"Everything's political. I pay attention, like A.R. taught me. I try to get my head around why tobacco is a legal drug and alcohol is illegal. It's politics. Politics and money. Why is betting on a hand of cards illegal and betting on a stock legal? Why can a bank take away a guy's house if he doesn't pay the mortgage, but it's illegal for me to charge a little *viggorish* on a private loan? And why are laws enforced sometimes and not other times?"

"The politicians, right? That's why we have elections, right?"

"It should be. But because Hoover will never have to answer to a President to keep his job, he's outside of ordinary politics. If he starts coming after people like me, people making money off Prohibition, and maybe some

104

other things, he would try the same thing, deportations and all."

We started walking back toward the beach end of the pier. Sam didn't seem to be in any hurry. I always liked listening to him; even as a kid, he had ideas.

He said, "You have to work with politicians. Look at Atlantic City. Nobody has ever been arrested for gambling or for drinking in this town. The law is one thing, how it gets enforced is what somebody like me has to understand, and that's politics. But Nucky, who's as good a politician as I've ever known, is really upset about this guy Hoover."

He flipped his cigarette butt over the rail and into the sea. "Arnold Rothstein, of blessed memory, was a genius for operating with the New York government, city and state. I try to follow his example. He had all the gossip, knew all the politicians. They watched out for him and he watched out for them. That's what he taught me. That's how power works. God, I miss that man."

Sam leaned his elbows on the top rail and looked out over the ocean. I stood and joined him, enjoying a view up the beach from that spot where the waves start to form, where they begin to rise up and roll. Parallel to the pier, a mile up the beach to the east, a long rock jetty protected the sand on the tip of Absecon Island from the tidal erosion at the mouth of the inlet. A tower, a navigation beacon, stood high and firm against the waves at the end of the jetty.

Quite soon, quite unexpectedly, I'd watch that light grow small as I stood on a weathered deck on an old boat headed out to sea.

Sam said, "Lately, Nucky and I, and some other men in our business, have been trying to do something new. We're trying to organize. It might actually work. You know, cooperate, agree on some people who can settle things for everyone's benefit when different groups might want a piece of the same action. We've been holding meetings. We had a big one here in Atlantic City just this Spring. That's why I've been in town so much lately."

"You mean gangs from different cities?"

"Exactly. Why should we be shooting each other? There's always a way to make deal."

"So that's it," I said. "This business about going after Hoover, it's because of this national organization you're talking about. Right?"

"Now you've got it," said Sam. "That's it. If we are going to operate across state lines, then we have to worry about the Federal Government. In most of the states, we can deal with the politicians. They come looking for us! But Federal is a different story. After the last election, Hoover was appointed. There has never been such a thing as a *permanent* director of the Federal Investigations Bureau before. I see it as an opportunity. I think we could make him part of the solution."

"By golly," I said. I was impressed that little Sam Brodsky from the Bronx, my friend, should be involved in such a big deal. And I finally understood the logic of going after Hoover, who was in a unique position to do them tremendous harm. But, if they could get him on their side, he could do them tremendous good. A way to do that was blackmail. "Holy mackerel," I said.

Sam laughed. "Yeah. It's a big deal. There's a lot riding on this, and not just for now, but for as long as he wants to keep his job."

"Do you think you can trust these other guys? The ones from other states?"

"We'll see. Most of us agree that we have to change. All of this shooting and blood… it's just plain stupid. We are trying to put a lid on the goons. It's like I told you that night we had dinner at Babette's, we're trying to give people some way to solve a problem without killing each other. It's bad for business. That's part of what this about."

"Your own justice system."

"Exactly. Ours, not J. Edgar Hoover's. And it makes sense, since we operate outside the regular law anyway."

"And now I'm in the middle of all that."

"Right smack dab," said Sam.

We strolled back to *Steel Pier Memories*. Sam stopped walking, lit another Chesterfield, and we stood watching our women in *Memories*. Helen was standing behind the little counter that I had built, eyeing the trade. She spotted us and waved. Pauline was leaning against the counter, licking an ice cream cone. Ida and Anne were deep in conversation, sitting on the two chairs I had set up for portraits. Apparently, Ida had found the connection.

"Nice place, Al. I'm happy for you. I hope you do well, *kaynahora*." That's Yiddish for, "Evil eye, stay away!" It's like saying, "No jinx."

"*Kaynahora*," I said.

Cold Feet

Hoover was scheduled to arrive late on Wednesday, May 30th. I intended to be waiting in the blind when he began his four-night hotel stay - his suite was booked through Sunday afternoon. I intended to spend Wednesday morning finishing preparations on the pier, shutter the stall early in the afternoon, and walk to the Ritz Carlton before three o'clock, the earliest check-in time.

Ida, Gabriel and the girls would arrive by train Wednesday evening and be on the pier bright and early to open up for business on the 31st. Ida and I had concocted a story to explain my absence on the big day – a big out of town wedding for which I had been committed for months and absolutely had to do. Gabriel and the girls bought it. We'd spent several days getting them ready and I wasn't worried about their ability to launch *Steel Pier Memories*.

Around noon on Wednesday, as I was finishing some darkroom plumbing, Dixon and Whitehead arrived for their promised visit.

I was not surprised to see them, although I had hoped that they would forget about me, that they would decide that the innocuous photographer was not worth a visit sixty miles away from their Philadelphia office, that they had better things to do with their time. Sam had reassured me that their interest was in Mike, that the Irishman was their focus, not me. Why would they waste their time?

"Mr. Rubin," said Whitehead. "It's nice to see you again."

"Likewise," I lied.

"I hope this is a good time," said Dixon.

"Not so good, actually," I said. "I'm busy. Tomorrow's the big day for us. Our first day. Tomorrow we open up for business and I got lots to do."

Whitehead said, "This shouldn't take very long. What can you tell us about Sam Brodsky?"

Dixon uncapped his pen and took a little notebook from the inside pocket of his suit. I noticed that he was wearing some kind of leather harness under his jacket.

"Like what? What's to tell?"

"Have you seen him lately?"

So, there it was. I could tell them no, but what if, somehow, they knew that Sam and his fiancée had paid us a visit on Saturday? What if they had people watching Sam and knew that we had spent an hour in conversation.

"He came by for a visit. Him and his fiancée."

They looked at each other. Dixon smiled just a bit. Whitehead said, "Yes, that's very interesting. When did this take place?" he asked.

So I explained that Sam brought his fiancée out to the pier last Saturday and that we had a nice family get-together, a chance for everybody to get acquainted. I overwhelmed them with meaningless information, gossip. I went into lots of detail about Anne and Sam's wedding plans. Dixon took notes, once or twice asking me to repeat something. I pictured him wearing his banker's suit at a typewriter transposing notes on catering to an official page for insertion into the Al Rubin file in a huge room full of tall, metal file cabinets in the basement of Hoover's building in Washington. Would he make a carbon copy to put in the Sam Brodsky folder? Would he place Sam's copy in an identical gray file cabinet many rows over? When I started talking about the wedding *hors d'oeuvre* menu, Whitehead decided to change the subject.

"Have you heard from your friend Mike Finnerty?" he asked. Dixon flipped to a blank page. Why should I have disappointed those men? I was a solid citizen. I would help them fill their files.

"No," I said. "I have not seen Mike since the shooting, and I am starting to worry. He used to have a girl friend, you know, in Philadelphia. Her name was Beatrice Cornell. But she got sick with the tuberculosis and died at the Mitchell Sanitarium. If she was still alive, I bet he would be with her right now. Such a shame, a beautiful young woman. That Mitchell place was very nice. For women only, you know. I went with Mike to visit once and it was so sad. He truly cared for her. Maybe even they would have gotten married. We drove out there in his first car. I'll never forget the day. He wasn't a very good driver and it was a used car, a *Reo* I think, and he had trouble starting it when we wanted to leave. Something called a magneto. It was a good thing that they had a man at the sanitarium who knew something about cars, because I sure don't; Mike certainly didn't. But it all worked out. He kept that car for a good long while. Come to think of it, I don't know what he's driving these days."

I gave them some of my good opinions about cars. They seemed to think that they had collected enough information for the files as I explained my certainty that the American automobile industry would soon find a way to cool people in the summer just as they had found a way to put heaters in cars.

Dixon closed his notebook. Whitehead said, "Do you still have my card, Mr. Rubin?"

"Yes, yes," and I removed the card from my wallet to show them.

"Be sure to give us a call if you happen to run into Finnerty.".

"So, you won't be coming next Wednesday?"

"Probably not," said Dixon.

I walked with them to the center of the midway and watched them head toward The Boardwalk entrance.

§

It was time to go. I turned off the lights in *Memories*, brought the lattice security gate down, and settled into the portrait chair that faced the midway. I felt the rumble of The Whip through the deck boards, heard the calliope's "Daring Young Man on the Flying Trapeze." I lit a cigarette, and allowed myself one last chance to change my mind.

I was about to do something that could ruin me if it went wrong. I had spent twenty-six years building a life in America and I was putting myself in a position to lose it all.

I was eighteen-years-old in 1903 when I said goodbye to my parents on the platform at Ungvar. Ahead of me was a four-hundred-mile train ride to Odessa, three days on a ship that would sail down the Black Sea, through the Dardanelles, and across the Mediterranean to Marseilles. Then I would board an overnight train to Le Havre, where I handed over my ticket for six days in the steerage section of an Atlantic freighter. I had been excited through the entire trip, looking forward to change, wait-ing for the new life I'd find in America. I had given little thought to what I was leaving behind – it wasn't a good life. Unless you were a rich man's son or a university-trained professional man, America was the place for you. Everybody knew that.

But I didn't have any idea of who I wanted to become. I was adrift, unformed, a poorly educated young man from an out-of-the-way town in Central Europe.

Like most immigrants, I had not expected America to be so difficult. I lived in a Bowery tenement, four flights up, in two rooms with an ever-changing group of men. The memories had merged and blurred: arguments, rusty cold water, rotting garbage, whores, unwashed roommates; and cold nights trudging to the high school for English classes. My first job was in a junkyard where I built little piles of nuts, bolts, screws and washers for re-sale. I was paid a penny for every five pounds. Then I moved up, taking one of those sweatshop pants cutter jobs. I never told Sam that we worked seven days a week, not six, often sixteen hours long, not twelve, that we worked until we couldn't stand, that we slept in shifts on cots, and went back to work.

The first year or so, liberated from parents and the narrow-minded neighbors in our tiny *shtetl* community, I had been the kind of person I would not want my daughters to meet. I drifted from one lousy job to another. I ate in saloons. I drank too much beer. I got into alley fights over pennies. I certainly did not see myself as a busi-nessman with a family. In those days I did not believe I had any chance of becoming the sort of person who owned a house or had a family. I don't even recall want-ing that kind of life.

Smushy Abramowitz taught me how to box. I used to be a sparring partner for his stable of Bowery boxers. Smushy managed a string of Jewish guys who fought for prize money all over New York back in the aughts. De-pending on the size of the prize, Smushy would keep up to half. He wanted me to box for prizes, saying that I would have, without any shadow of a doubt, become the New York middleweight champion. He bought me din-ners and introduced me to good-looking women. I was flattered, but I turned him down. Smushy told all the guys that they were going to be champions. Besides, the two-bits a round he paid me as a sparring partner was guaranteed.

Looking back, watching the sparse foot traffic on the midway, I remembered that I had no ambitions of any kind. Then I met Ida.

She was only fourteen when she came from Ruthenia in 1905. I knew some of her relatives. Her older brother ran a corner store in Hell's Kitchen where she worked from the day she got off the boat. We were introduced in 1909 and immediately went crazy. We got married just a few months later, because it was the only way we could get the kind of privacy we needed.

Besides her brother in New York, Ida had a brother and two sisters who had made a life for themselves in Philadelphia. They pooled some of their savings and bought us a storefront photo studio in West Philadelphia. We knew nothing about photography, but it was an established little business that had been available from the widow at a bargain price. A couple of cameras in a hole-in-the-wall storefront was a wedding gift from my in-laws.

I remember that we survived the first few months in Philadelphia eating at the tables of her relatives. Then, after we started breaking even, we moved into a one room apartment near the studio. The second year, the business was slightly profitable. As I got more skillful, profit became more predictable. During our third year, I paid back Ida's relatives for their small investment in the business.

During those first years in Philadelphia, I started to believe that I might be able to accomplish something. Those early years, building the business, I started to feel proud of myself. It occurred to me, as I watched the sparse pedestrian traffic on the midway, that I was as proud of how I had built the business as the business itself. I had been honest and straightforward in my dealings.

But doing the Hoover job was forcing me to give up the smug comfort of scrupulous honesty. By the time the long Decoration Day weekend would be over, I would be a different, less admirable, sort of person. That would be the cost of the exercise, no matter how it turned out.

Helen was born in 1911. Pauline was born in 1913. In 1920 we took out a huge mortgage and bought the property on Chester Avenue in Southwest Philadelphia. By then, I had forgotten how to be the tough guy; I wanted to be like everyone else.

I sat in the shadows as people walked past on the midway. Why had I put myself in this situation? I feared that when the Hoover escapade was over, no matter how it would end, I wouldn't like myself. But, then if I was such an honest guy, why had I taken such delight in deceiving Dixon and Whitehead?

Because it's fun to have secrets. I was enjoying my-self. I was intrigued by the technical challenge of taking pictures in low light, true. But more, I was enjoying the secrecy, the newness, and the risk.

Yes, I wanted to make the leap from 'a comfortable living' to 'doing very well.' *Steel Pier Memories* would pay off, I was sure. That little business would clear three or four times as much in a summer as the Chester Avenue studio made in a year. I would be able to afford real col-lege for the girls. I would make stock market investments like the big *mahoffs* who are officers of the synagogue. I would buy a new car every year. I would buy real oil paintings, like Sam. I would go to Paris with Ida and teach her about *chateaubriand* and champagne.

But, until I visited Sam in his penthouse, I had never desired those things. I liked my life as it was. I didn't feel poor or deprived. I loved my *De Soto*, paid all my bills every month. I was proud of *Albert Photos* and of the honest business I did, which, every year, little by little, got bigger. The art photographs I took for myself kept me interested in my craft. I was fine. What the hell was I do-ing? What was pulling me?

And what about what I'd lose, what about the effect on my family? If I did get caught, I wouldn't worry about Helen and Pauline. The mortgage on the building on Chester Avenue was paid off. Ida could run the busi-ness as well as I. Helen would pull her weight. Those two would be okay; embarrassed by my crime, maybe, but

117

okay. Would Pauline be all right without me to keep her from trouble? I didn't know. Ida was able to control her better than I, anyway.

Sad, but true, Ida would find somebody else.

So, those were the risks. Not so bad.

On the good side, if nothing went wrong, my family and I would be better off, and I would be connected to powerful friends. It was a good gamble, I thought, especially since I believed that I'd made a good plan and had taken all possible precautions. I told myself that I was a guy who knows how to manage, who knows how to think on his feet, how to deal with trouble if it happens to come along.

As for the morality of it, I rationalized that Sam and Nucky were right, that nobody in government should have Hoover's power. By weakening him, I'd be strengthening America.

I stood and stretched, feeling the strength return to my legs and shoulders. I reopened the lattice gate and locked it from the outside. I strode down the midway, excited, feeling much as I had a quarter century before, when I stepped aboard the train to Odessa.

PART TWO

First Night

No one was in the corridor when I stepped inside the linen closet and closed the door behind me. A housekeeper or a nosey hotel guest would have detected nothing out of the ordinary had they opened that door. They would have seen shelves stacked with sheets and towels and a floor cluttered with buckets and cleaning supplies. Such a person, I hoped, would catch a whiff of ammonia and close the door at once, having no idea that the linen closet was the anteroom to the blind. I unlatched the false back and swung it slowly open, careful not to send the linens tumbling.

Inside what had once been Suite 1202 of the *Ritz Carlton Hotel,* I ducked under the blackout drape in the front room and peered through the spy hole in the wall. I did the same with the drape and hole in the bedroom wall. Both rooms next door were as I had left them – unoccupied. I had time to kill.

I opened the French door and stood on the narrow balcony, heard the sound of the waves breaking on the beach and smelled the tang of brine and sand. There were no lifeguards in the plywood stands; they would not begin their duties until the following day, Decoration Day, the official opening of Atlantic City's summer season. There were people out there, nevertheless, enjoying the sunshine and the sea breeze, most fully-clothed, some throwing pieces of driftwood for their dogs. I hoped that it might all be over that night, before a lifeguard blew a whistle. I took an ashtray to the windowsill and pulled up a chair to wait.

It was late in the afternoon when I heard the passenger elevator clang open in the hallway. I went under the drape in the front room in time to see the door of the suite opening. A bellhop came in, followed by a Negro porter with two big suitcases. Next in was a Negro in a chauffeur's uniform carrying a smaller suitcase and a briefcase. J. Edgar Hoover entered last.

I recognized him from a photograph in a Washington Post article that I had found at the library. It was a long story about a 34-year-old man from Washington D.C. who had risen like a star in the Federal Government, having been appointed as the permanent Director of the Investigations Bureau of the United States Department of Justice. Folks in Washington, apparently, thought J. Edgar Hoover was terrific.

It was from that article that I learned that he had gone to a military high school in Washington D.C. and also to a college in Washington D.C. and to a night school to become a lawyer. His tailored suit was cut a bit tightly, almost like a cadet's uniform. He was trim, compact and controlled. He had dark, arched eyebrows and large, wide set eyes that dominated his face.

I had installed false heating registers, two in each room, near the ceiling, so that I could hear. Hoover gave coins to the bellhop and the porter and sent them on their way.

"Let's just get unpacked, Pierre, and you'll be done for the day," he said to the chauffeur. "Is your sister expecting you?" I had no trouble hearing what he was saying.

"I expect so," said the man. "I sent her a letter. Then, this afternoon, before we left D.C., I sent her a telegram. I said I'd be stopping by whenever I was done for the day."

They went into the bedroom of Suite 1200 – I followed into the bedroom of the blind. Through the spy hole, I watched them transfer clothes from two of the suitcases into closets and dressers.

"I take it your sister doesn't have a telephone," Hoover said. "What if I should need you?"

"I can give you her address, I guess. If you really need me, you could find me there. Otherwise, I'll just come by tomorrow morning. What time?" He scribbled an address on a piece of hotel stationery.

Hoover looked at the sheet of paper when it was handed to him, clearly unhappy with the idea that his man would not be within hailing distance. "Just leave it on the desk. Give me a call from the lobby tomorrow at eight o'clock," he said. With that, the man named Pierre left Hoover's rooms.

Alone, the Director took a small address book from the inside of his jacket and went to the telephone on the nightstand by the bed. After the hotel operator connected him to the local number, he made a dinner reservation for two under the name of Anderson. I thought, perhaps, that the person with whom he was to have dinner was named Anderson.

Then he asked the operator to place a call to a number in Washington. "Hello, Mother," he said. "No, it was good that I took the car. Clement and I were able to get some work done in the back seat. It was very pleasant... No, Mother, Pierre's an excellent driver. No, I don't know where he learned about cars... I guess it is a bit unusual, but he's not a fool... There's a parade in the morning, on the Boardwalk. I'll be sitting with Senator Edge on the reviewing stand... He's the Senator from New Jersey, the one who invited me... Absolutely. I already have... Sunday, after you get back from church... Yes, Mother," he said, and hung the ear piece in its cradle.

I watched him hoist the third suitcase onto the bed, insert a key, and unlock the latches. He carefully removed a large sheet of tissue paper, lifted a pair of lady's bloomers and held them at arm's length to admire them.

I pulled out from under the dark curtain. It was one thing to think about invading a person's privacy, as I had been doing for more than a month. Doing it, I had just learned, was a different matter. I returned to my chair by the window, lit a cigarette and reconsidered my approach to the job. I really did not want to look anymore. Spying made me feel unclean, no matter how innocent the activities I was observing.

I decided that there was no need to watch him all the time. I would just take a peek every once in awhile. I'd know whether he had company by the sound of voices. That's when I would look, my finger on the shutter. In the meanwhile, I'd wait and read the library book I'd brought with me.

The camera equipment case sat on the floor next to the connecting doorway between the front and back rooms of the blind. The camera cases were in it and the contact prints from the pictures I'd taken of the girls and Mrs. Krusciewski at Memories. I had a magnifying glass and intended to study the prints for flaws, to see whether I needed to make any adjustments to the camera settings on the pier.

I had six pre-sensitized rolls of film inside the equipment case along with the instruction books and carrying cases that had come with the *Rolleiflex*es. I had practiced loading the cameras in the dark. If I was to need more than the 12 exposures that were on each of the rolls in the cameras, I could go into the bathroom, close the door, place towels across the bottom to seal out all the light and replace the spools of film in a matter of minutes.

I had gotten to the second chapter of a best seller by Sinclair Lewis when I heard the elevator doors clang open and closed in the corridor. Back to work.

Through my spy hole in the front room, I saw Hoover switch on a lamp and open the door for a tall man carrying a closed cocktail shaker in one hand and two cocktail glasses by their stems between the fingers of his other hand.

"Oh, Clement, you devil," said Hoover.

The man named Clement came in, grinning. Hoover ducked his head out the door and looked both ways along the corridor before he closed it.

"Shall we?" asked Clement. He took the glasses and shaker to a bar cabinet against the far wall and set them down.

"Oh, I suppose there's no harm in it. This is, after all, Atlantic City. What did you bring us?" Hoover switched on another lamp.

"Manhattans," said Clement as he poured. He was a tall man wearing a light-colored suit with narrow pin stripes set far apart. They sat on the sofa. I depressed the shutter as they sat next to each other with their glasses raised. "Cheers," said Clement. Quickly, I wound the film to '2.'

"So, have you made any progress on the Johnson tap?" asked Hoover.

"We put a woman who reports to Whitehead at the phone company switchboard. She will take notes on calls coming into the hotel to Johnson. That's easy. Calls coming out are harder. Unless Johnson announces himself, she won't know whether it's him, one of the guests, or one of the business offices. Our problem is that the guy owns the hotel. Not on paper. But this place is Johnson's."

"Take your time," said Hoover. "We must be exceptionally careful with this operation. Assign Dixon and Whitehead to the problem. Let's see what they come up with."

"Why is this guy so important?" asked Clement. "Surely he's not a subversive. He's not a criminal, is he?"

Hoover sipped the Manhattan. "Certainly he is. He is a particularly well-connected gangster masquerading as a politician." Taking another sip, he continued. "So, we know he is a crook. Every newspaper in the country knows it. They glorify him, for God's sake. He's the 'Czar of the Ritz,' is he not? But my chief concern is not his involvement with gangsters; it's his involvement with legitimate politicians and public officials. I have reason to believe that he is in the center of a web of corruption that may go very high.

"I'll tell you why," said the Director of the Investigations Bureau. "I was once ordered to stay away from Atlantic City. It was 1923. We had begun a very promising investigation of illegal immigrants working on the entertainment piers along the East Coast. I personally wrote to this Enoch Johnson, reaching out to him for assistance with the investigations in Atlantic City. I had previously written to the Mayor and the District Attorney and gotten no response. Nigel Hawes, you know him, he's from somewhere in South Jersey, he suggested that this Johnson was the real Boss of the town.

"Three days after I sent Johnson the letter, Palmer summoned me to his office and told me to back off investigations in Atlantic City. Remember, this was the year before I became Acting Director, so I was still following orders. 'Why?' I asked. Palmer wouldn't tell me, but I'm pretty sure that this Johnson was able to pressure him, and I think I know how.

"Here's the interesting fact. Woodrow Wilson was in Palmer's office earlier that morning. Everyone in the building was talking about it. Wilson was from New Jersey. I can't be certain, of course, but I suspect that Wilson's visit was prompted by my letter to Johnson."

Clement took his empty glass to the bar and poured himself another Manhattan. Hoover waved his glass for a refill and Clement obliged. "Fascinating," said Clement. "Wilson wasn't even President anymore."

"No. But he did live in the District. His wife hated New Jersey. Mother told me."

"So you think this man has enough influence to get an ex- President to do his bidding?"

"I do. Then there's the curious coincidence of my invitation to participate in Decoration Day commemorations." Hoover paused here.

"Oh, please, go on," said Clement.

Hoover smiled, appreciating Clement's attention. "I got the invitation to attend these festivities within a day of having asked Wally Edge about Johnson. It was outside the Senate hearing room back in early March. I was on my way out, after testifying on the budget for Fiscal '31, when I ran into Senator Edge, who is a junior member of the Committee. He shook my hand and complimented me on my testimony. He appreciated my knowledge of the details and my sense of the mission. 'I'm just doing my duty as I see it,' I told him. He was still shaking my hand, said he wished more of the officials who come before the committee are as well prepared as I. He continued to shake my hand. I managed to extricate myself and I thanked him for the kind words. Then, I asked him about Enoch Johnson. You know me, Clement. I never forget. What happened with Palmer still rankles. Who better than the Senator from New Jersey to give me a little insight into a man who can get presidents to act for him? So, I say, fishing, 'And how's my friend Enoch?'

First, he doesn't know who I'm talking about. Then he says, 'Oh, you mean Nucky. Nucky Johnson?' The very same, I say. 'Fine, fine. Nucky's very fine, I'm sure. I'll tell him you inquired.' The very next afternoon, the Senator's hand written invitation to enjoy New Jersey's hospitality is delivered, by courier, to my office. I'm offered this lovely suite, an invitation to review the parade, to attend the Grand Army of the Republic's Ball to inaugurate the new Convention Hall, and to have a private dinner with the Senator and a few friends.

"Normally, I would decline. You know me, Clement. I never accept favors – the slippery slope and all that. Then, after I thought it over, I changed my mind. This Nucky Johnson is a man we need to know more about. Palmer is gone. The days when the Bureau kowtows to political bosses are over. We certainly don't need a political boss just a hundred and fifty miles from Washington who thinks he can say 'no' to the Federal Government! I'm convinced that the entertainment piers are havens for immigrant Communists and Anarchists and every sort of subversive. And, I'll bet you dollars to doughnuts that the piers are being used in the smuggling rackets, for rum running. So, you see, Clement, I'm really here on the Government's business."

"So, you want to find evidence? To bring charges?" asked Clement.

"Charges? Clement, Clement, Clement, my dear fellow, we're a long way from even thinking about charges. We investigate! That's our job. But who knows what valuable tidbits we might discover with a little bit of discreet eavesdropping? I know that we absolutely cannot abide the idea of politicians thwarting federal investigations.

It's a new day! Personally, I would be happy if we found a little something to hold in reserve should the need ever arise.

"These Manhattans are very good, by the way. Thank you."

Clement said, "I brought all the fixings down in my luggage. Except the ice. I had them send that up to my room. I certainly didn't want to have to go looking for an out-of-town supplier! Too risky. For you, I mean."

"Oh, Clement, whatever would I do without you?" Hoover drained his glass. "Are we set to go? We have a reservation at the Entertainers Club for eight o'clock. That's what you're wearing?"

"Let me just freshen up a bit. You look very nice, by the way," said Clement. They rose from the couch. As they stood looking at each other, I clicked the shutter on the second exposure."

"Thank you," said Hoover. "I'll use the bathroom after you."

Hoover turned on the radio and looked for a station, eventually turning up the volume on a Rudy Vallee song. They took turns using the bathroom. When Hoover came out, he said something that I couldn't hear above the radio advertisement, a jingle about how terrific it is to bake with *Fleischman's Yeast*. As they left the suite, Hoover switched off the radio and the lights. I heard the metallic rattling of the elevator gate opening and closing.

129

The Sinclair Lewis best seller was called *Elmer Gantry*. I love his books and found myself happily immersed in the world of professional Christians. Reb Mendel, the *cheder* master in the village where I grew up in Ungvar, never talked about Hell, so I was asking myself whether Jewish people are supposed to believe in Hell and Heaven when I heard the elevator return to the twelfth floor. It was almost midnight.

Back under the drape in the front room, I saw the door to 1200 open and a hand reach in to turn on the switch for the ceiling light. Hoover was not alone: Clement was still with him. They went right into the bedroom where Hoover turned on the bedside lamp. Clement started to pull the drapes closed across the French door that opened to the little patio.

Hoover said, "Leave it open. Sea breeze, you know." This was the best news, it meant that the morning light would shine right on the bed.

Again, they took turns using the bathroom. They talked to each other through the open bathroom door. Hoover wanted to know whether Clement liked the music at the Entertainers Club. Clement wanted to know whether Hoover liked the food. They both liked everything. They'd had a wonderful time.

Hoover came out of the bathroom wearing a negligee.

He sat on the edge of the bed and switched off the nightstand lamp, turning their bedroom completely dark before I could get a picture. My workday was over.

On the couch in the front room, I finished most of the book. Eventually I fell into a troubled sleep with the novel on my chest. At some small hour, having been awakened by a nightmare about a sunrise, I stumbled into the other room and got into the bed. As dawn started to light the room, I fell asleep again.

Decoration Day

A lot of sunlight was coming in around the edges of the curtain when the phone ringing in Hoover's suite awakened me. I looked at my watch and saw that it was a few minutes before eight o'clock. Decoration Day.

Through the bedroom peephole, I saw that the bed was empty. Hoover, standing by the desk, wearing the negligee, held the telephone to his ear. "Come up at eight thirty," he said, and hung up. The curtain was still wide open; the brilliant sun and reflections off the sea and sand were flooding the room in a clear light.

Hoover disappeared into the bathroom. I took a quick peek at the front room and saw that it was empty. Clement must have returned to his room before the phone rang. With half an hour to clean myself up, I stretched, rolled my shoulders, scratched my scalp and went into the bathroom. As I washed up, I was angry at myself for having slept through the dawn and the morning light. But, I reassured myself, it was only Friday and Hoover would not check out for two more days. I would have other opportunities.

I was dressed and ready just in time. The elevator gate clanged open at exactly 8:30. Hoover, now wearing trousers and a shirt, opened the door for Pierre, who took a couple of steps into the room and scanned the walls. He stepped past his employer and came directly to the mirror. Startled, I took a step backward. It was obvious that he was not looking at his reflection; he was inspecting the mirror itself.

"Boss," he said. "I got to tell you about what my brother-in-law Charles told me this morning at breakfast. He works at this hotel."

I did not need to hear another word.

From the first, I had considered the possibility that a quick exit might be necessary and that I had to be careful to bring nothing to the blind that could be associated with me. I had put nothing in drawers. I had just brought a change of underwear for three days, a fresh shirt, and a shaving kit. I dashed back into the bathroom and grabbed my shaving kit, leaving yesterday's underwear on the tile where I had dropped it before stepping into the shower. In the bedroom, I grabbed the valise. With no tie or collar on my shirt, I pulled on my suit jacket. I was about to open the false partition when I remembered the library book. I spun and ran back to retrieve it and drop it into the valise. I rotated in the middle of the room, looking for anything else that they might use to find me.

The cameras! The serial numbers! I reached under the drapery, grabbed one of *Rolleiflex* cameras and pushed it into the valise. I should go back for the other one? No time! Anything in the equipment case? I didn't think so, I hoped not. I swung the false partition open, spilling towels onto the floor of the blind. I cracked open the door to the hallway. Seeing no one, I entered the corridor and closed the "Linens" door cautiously behind me.

I headed down the corridor, away from Suite 1200, toward the corner that turns to the fire exit and the service elevator. Just a few more steps and I'd be out of sight. As I made the turn, I heard a door being opened. It was like a kick in the ass. I ran to the fire exit at full speed. As I yanked the steel door open, I heard a voice, Hoover's, ring out, "Son of a bitch!" He must have opened the "Linens" door.

As fast as I could, I skipped down the gloomy stairwell. There were two flights of cement stairs for each floor. By the light of red bulbs in steel safety cages at each landing, I saw floor numbers stenciled on the fire doors. "11," "10,"

My shoes barely touched the cement. I went faster, finding a rhythm. A door opened above. A shout echoed, "Go down. Go down! I'll go up." I opened the door to the sixth floor, hoping that the pneumatic closer completed its job before Pierre, whose footsteps I clearly heard, reached it.

I walked quickly away from the fire door and turned the corner. There, I stopped to catch my breath. The corridor was empty, no sound behind me. I knelt and opened the valise to retrieve my starched collar and bow tie from the bottom. Hastily, without the benefit of a mirror, I finished getting dressed in the hallway of the sixth floor of the *Ritz Carlton Hotel*. With the tie on, feeling respectable, the fear ebbed a little. I walked to the passenger elevator and pushed the call button.

The elevator doors opened immediately; apparently I had caught the car on its descent. The operator pulled the lattice gate open and greeted me with, "Lobby, sir?"

I, the carefree hotel guest, smiled. "Yes, thank you," I said.

Hoover, without a tie and collar, without a jacket, did not look as respectable as I. He was agitated, breathing deeply, nostrils flaring, impatient and unhappy that the operator had paused during the elevator's descent to pick up another passenger.

"Good morning," I said. Hoover did not appear to hear me. I turned my back to face the front of the car and willed myself to be calm. Once in the lobby, I headed toward The Boardwalk exit. As I put my back to the revolving door, I saw Hoover with both fists on the front desk. The wide-eyed clerk was paying close attention.

I made a left onto The Boardwalk and went east toward *Steel Pier*. I'd walked about a block and was in front of the Convention Hall when I spotted a good place from which to scan the foot traffic, to see if I was being followed. I walked across the strange space that they'd made of the Boardwalk in front of the enormous, new building. Up to my left was a patriotic storm of red, white and blue. Bunting was draped over the railings in front of the reviewing stand, a long row of flags hung across the entire front of the Hall. Bleachers had been erected in sections between tall, be-flagged columns.

That area of the Boardwalk had been permanently expanded with a concrete pavement curving over the beach toward the sea in an arc mimicking the curve of the vast roof. A double row of concrete columns had been built along the curved edge of arc to form a colonnade. I chose a column to lean against, lit a cigarette, and watched the sparse, early morning crowd.

The parade ground in front of the Convention Hall is startling after the penny-ante game stalls, the schlock shops and hot dog stands that line the boardwalk on either side of it. George Hamid and the Chamber of Commerce had, no doubt, been trying to achieve monumental grandeur with the parade ground and the colonnade. To me, it just seemed pompous and out of place.

I returned to the familiar Boardwalk, the real Atlantic City, at the east end of the parade ground. Vendors and hucksters were preparing for the parade crowd, the first of the 1929 summer season. I felt a kinship with each proprietor as I passed the stalls and storefronts. I was an insider, a man with a business on The Boardwalk who was going to make a lot of money that summer because the economy was booming. The stock market was setting records every day, everybody had a job and money to spend.

I picked a telephone booth from a row along the railing near the *Steel Pier*, fished a nickel out of my pocket and called the *Ritz*. The hotel's operator didn't want to believe that Mr. Kessel would really, truly like to talk to me. "He's very busy right now," she said.

"I'm aware, lady. Believe me, I'm aware. Tell Louie that Al is on the line. He will talk to me."

I waited, watching two lifeguards move their rowboat down toward the water's edge on a pair of rollers. I had to put another nickel in before Louie finally came to the phone. He sounded calm. "Al, what the hell happened?"

"Somebody who works at your hotel, somebody named Charles, who is the brother in law of a man who works for Hoover — that's what happened. Pierre, that's Hoover's man, he came to work this morning, and the first thing he did, the very first thing, was tell Hoover about the mirrors. I left in a hurry when I heard that, let me tell you."

"Oho! That's what it was. Charles, you say?"

"Yes, Charles Henderson, your hotel carpenter, is the brother-in- law of Pierre."

"Okay, I guess I will have to talk with this Charles. I'm glad you got out in time. Hoover is treating 1202 like he owns it. He is saying that I can't touch nothing. Hah! He's got a guy in 1202 right now, standing guard. I don't know where he got him from."

"It's probably this guy Clement, the one who was with him last night. He's staying at the hotel, too."

138

An operator interrupted us to say that she wanted me to please deposit another five cents. I dropped my last nickel in the slot.

"Hoover says to me to stay out until his team is finished. To me! In my own hotel! He's waiting for people to come from Philly. They are bringing their own cameras to take pictures. They are going to find fingerprints. Meanwhile, all I am supposed to do is watch with my hands in my pockets. Nucky says the horse is out of the barn, to let him have his way. Hoover, he don't have the right to do it, but Nucky says it's good to make him feel like he's in charge. It pisses me off, let me tell you!"

"Fingerprints! I never thought of fingerprints! What shall I do?"

"Has anybody ever taken your fingerprints?"

"No. I don't think so."

"Then relax. They won't have nothing to match with. I'll keep you out of this."

"Thanks, Louie. What about Nucky?" I ask.

"Oh boy! Hoover is wanting to see him. I had to wake him up, which is always very bad idea. He hates it. I tell him that Hoover finds room 1202, but that nobody is in it. Nobody knows where you are. I tell him that Hoover is screaming for somebody's blood. Nucky listens, he calls Hoover a bad name, then he goes back to sleep."

"He really went back to sleep?"

"Yep!"

"Louie, you need to talk to him. Hoover has some-body listening to Nucky's telephone. He can listen in to anybody. Maybe even this call."

"How do you know this?"

"Last night. He talked about it with his friend, how they do it."

Louie laughed. "I'll be damned. Nucky's gonna love that!"

"And listen, Louie, tell Nucky that Hoover is really out to get him."

"And they talk about this last night?"

"That's all they talked about."

"Okay. I will tell Nucky. Probably he will want to hear about this from you. Okay?"

"Of course. But, Louie, be sure to tell him that I am sorry. I just had to leave. I think if I stayed another se-cond they would have caught me."

"Yeah, yeah. You did the right thing. Now where do you go?"

"I guess I'll just go back to the pier. Go to work. Make some money."

Louie said, "That's good. Stay close. I will let you know when Nucky wants to talk to you. Until then, you should be careful," he said.

We had told Gabriel and the girls that I was going to be in Philadelphia for a big wedding. Ida played along, not batting an eye as I told them that the make-pretend wedding had been cancelled. At midday, after we let

Gabe and the girls go to watch the parade, I told Ida what had happened at the *Ritz*.

Ida hugged her arms and shook her head. "So it's over?" she said.

"Probably. But they have my equipment case and one of the cameras. And they will have my fingerprints. So, we'll see. But Louie says not to worry."

"Louie! Who is Louie!? Can he tell the federal government what to do? *Oy*, Al! What a mess."

I had to agree.

As soon as the Boardwalk parade was over, people bought tickets to the *Steel Pier* and we had more work than we could handle. A line formed of people who were willing to wait. When the girls came back from the parade, Ida told them how to keep people from getting angry: "We are so very sorry. Please be patient. Come back later." Most people weren't willing to wait long, but it didn't seem to matter, because there was always another customer, and another, and another. Hurray! I was thinking that I would have to set up at least one more camera. Gabriel had already reloaded a dozen film holders in the darkroom. It was terrific!

As much as I like Mike Finnerty, as worried as I had been about his welfare since the shooting, I was not glad to see him when he showed up. "Ida, how is the picture business? Albert, how is the picture business?"

"Hello, Mike. It's good to see you. Stick around for awhile," I said.

141

Mike came right next to me as I was peering through the viewfinder at a pretty girl with her head on the Miss America body. Quietly, he said, "Let's go. Hoover's men are on their way."

Ida was watching us as I took the picture. I took her aside and told her what Mike had just said. "You and the girls will have to do without me for awhile." I grabbed the valise from under the counter, where I'd put it after I had escaped from the hotel.

"Al! Where are you going?" demanded my wife. "*Now?* You can't leave *now*! How long will you be away? *Oy vay is mir*! Al! This is crazy!"

Pauline whined, "Daddy, where are you going?"

"Sorry, my dears, I think this is an emergency."

The midway was crowded with people moving, milling in every direction. "Ida, darling," yelled Mike over his shoulder. "I'll keep him safe. Don't worry."

As we shouldered through the crowd, above the piping calliope of the carousel and the thudding of hundreds of shoes on boards, in a cry that floated clearly above the rumbling sound of The Whip and the shrieks of its passengers, I heard my wife call out, "Don't worry?! Why should I worry?!"

Sweet Emma

In Atlantic City, if you were Mike Finnerty and you worked for Nucky Johnson's partner, you could park anywhere you wanted to. Mike's sparkling new Reo coupe was waiting on Virginia Avenue in the fire zone at the foot of the Boardwalk ramp. We jumped in and Mike tried to turn the car around quickly, but he had not mastered the U-turn − he went slowly in reverse, too fast forward. It took him three tries to get us pointed out toward Pacific Avenue. I was prepared to take off on foot if I saw tall men in dark suits.

"Nice car," I said.

"Brand new," he said. "I just picked it up. It's my second one of these."

"Your second '29 Reo?"

"Yep." I didn't ask − Mike was a guy who would have been better off holding reins instead of a steering wheel.

He crossed Pacific and went to Atlantic where he made a right, taking us east, toward the Inlet. We passed a group of men in military uniforms returning from the parade, carrying brass instruments, as we turned left onto Rhode Island Avenue.

"Good, you're taking me to my house." I said.

"Nope, I figger they know where you live. If they're not waiting for you now, they will be here soon enough. We're going a block or two farther on Rhode Island Avenue, to the docks, because we're getting on a boat."

"Stop here," I said, as we passed the house.

"No time," Mike said. "I think we need to stay ahead of these Hoover people. They think they are the Federal fuckin' Government."

We soon came to the fishing village two blocks north of 113 North Rhode Island Avenue. Mike tried to park. Finally, with the right front tire a foot from the curb, the right rear tire on the sidewalk, he considered the vehicle sufficiently parked to turn the motor off.

"Mike, do they know it was me in 1202? How would they know?" I asked as we were crossing the street. On the opposite sidewalk stood Atlantic City's fish market, a haphazard row of shanties with hanging scales out front next to tall, ice tables on which the catch had been laid. Hand-lettered signs showed the prices.

He said, "Hoover and his man, Clement Talbot, bullied the hotel workers who helped you set up. They said, 'It was this Jew photographer, a feller with brown hair, but not too much, who always wears ties, even to saw holes in walls.'

"I have a lot of hair! But how did they know to find me on the pier? The people at the hotel don't know anything about *Steel Pier Memories*," I said as we walked between two shacks.

"I don't know. Maybe you left something in the room?"

I had left the prints of the girls and Mrs. Krusciewski in the camera case, intending to study them for flaws while I wasn't watching through the spy holes. The pictures showed Atlantic City scenery. All they would have had to do was walk The Boardwalk until they found a shop with the same scenery.

"Damn!" I said. "I'm an idiot. I left a few contact prints with my scenery in the camera case. I'm an idiot!"

We were standing on the wharf behind the shacks.

"I've always know you're an idjit, but that's neither here nor there. They probably just put two and two together. They were looking for a photographer and they have been talking to you anyways. A couple of Federal agents paid you a visit in Philadelphia?"

"I told Sam all about it on Saturday. I'm sure he mentioned it to Nucky. I didn't tell them anything. I wouldn't. Sam knows that."

"What did you tell the G Men?"

"G Men? What's a G Man?"

Mike said, "A Government Man. That's what the papers call Hoover's people."

"Well, here's another bit of news. They came to see me again yesterday."

"What about?"

"You. And Sam. But I didn't say anything. I think I bored them to tears. I told them about your old girlfriend

145

and car troubles you used to have. I told them about Sam's wedding. Just bullshit. And, you should know, they are extremely interested in Mister Michael Finnerty. What's that about? What was that shooting about on the pier? They are definitely after *both* of us, now. So, I don't appreciate you talking as if this is all my doing!"

"You are absolutely correct. So, me pal, until we figure out our next move, we're going to be unavailable."

§

Sweet Emma was an ugly fishing boat. I was trying not to breathe through my nose as I stepped aboard. The boat was about fifty feet long, her stern wide and low. Dominating the middle of the deck was a white wheelhouse with rust stains dripping from blistered rivets and from the rungs welded to its side. Her prow jutted up to the height of the wheelhouse. The deck planks underfoot were worn gray, their grain open and rough.

Machine parts and a set of tools were spread around a man who rose from the peach crate he was using as a stool. "Mike," he said. "You're early."

"Captain, this is Albert Rubin. Al, this is Captain Jack DeWease."

The captain looked me over. I saw a momentary narrowing of his eyes – he didn't appear to like what he saw.

Mike explained, "Albert here, he's one of Sam's people. He will be with us for tonight."

DeWease checked a pocket watch. He said, "We have a good tide for another couple of hours." He looked at the sky. "Looks like it will be a good night for it. Water's pretty calm, no weather comin'. " He slid the watch back into the pocket of his soiled work pants, adjusted the billed cap on his head, and said, "I'll go get Billy and his pal. Make yourself a pot of coffee."

I followed Mike down a short ladder to cramped crew quarters. Faint light leaked into the cabin through grimy port holes. Four berths were attached to the hull, two on each side. Mike went to a latched cupboard and brought out a can of *Maxwell House*, filled a coffee pot from a tap at the bottom of a fresh-water tank, lit a burner on the cook stove, and set the pot on it to brew. Waiting for the coffee to percolate, I sat across from Mike at a scarred table in the middle of the cabin.

"Michael, what have I gotten myself into? What is this boat?"

"Believe it or not, this here is Sam's boat."

I could not form an image of the dapper little man aboard that craft. "Sam wouldn't set foot on a boat like this," I said.

"I think he did, but just the oncet to see where his money was going. He's got a few boats. A fleet, you might say."

"Rum runners?"

Michael laughed. "Your cousin, he's figured out that it's the cheapest, safest way to get the product. He doesn't have to pay off stevedores or pier owners or worry about Customs Agents who are, don't you know, generally more expensive than stevedores and pier owners. When the boats tie up, they unload right onto Sam's very own trucks, driven by Sam's very own teamsters. From the docks, they go all over, legal and aboveboard. Except for the cargo."

"Except for the cargo." I said, amazed at Mike's cavalier regard for the Volstead Act. "What if they stop the trucks or the boats?"

"It happens, but none of it's in Sam's name. He's got different ways that his old boss, Rothstein, showed him. Truth is, himself, Rothstein had set a lot of it up before he got himself killed. Mostly, what it is, is these corporations as the legal owners of the boats and everything. There's even warehouses. But Sam, he doesn't have his name *on* anything. *Sweet Emma*, don't you know, is owned by Something-Or-Other Transportation Incorporated. This used to be Jack DeWease's boat, entirely, until he had to give it up on account of some very big gambling debts. But, so long as he stays on Sam's good side, he still gets to captain this piece of *shite.* "

We'd taken metal cups of steaming coffee onto the deck. Noisy gulls were on the roofs and on the pilings, strutting around the shacks. A fishing boat, with buckets and crates stacked around its rails, was tied alongside the dock behind the *Sweet Emma*.

148

"Mike, are you going to tell me what happened on the pier? Why did Seamus get shot? Who was the man who shot him? Where did you go?"

"Al, if I don't tell you, it's for your own good."

"Ignorance is bliss, you mean?"

"There's that. But what if Hoover's men start to question you about it? If Albert Rubin doesn't know anything, then Albert Rubin has nothing to hide."

"They have already questioned me. Twice. Guess what? They don't care a thing about the shooting. They say it's local police business. But they *do* want to find you, sir. You know that you can trust me not to say anything. Not even to Ida."

"They didn't question you about the shooting?"

"They said it was none of their business. I got the strong impression that they were interested in you for other reasons. And something Hoover said last night lets me think it has to do with Irishmen without visas working on the *Steel Pier*. Am I right?"

Mike regarded me for a long moment. "A few of Sam's little boats carry merchandise out to the freighters," he said. "This here boat carries munitions. The freighter we're meeting tonight is going to drop an empty cargo net down to the *Sweet Emma*. Billy DeWease, Jack's boy, and his friend are going to fill the net with crates, each one containing four bolt-action Springfield M-1903 rifles. There are twenty-five such crates in the hold of this stout vessel, even as we speak. That's one

149

hundred U.S. Army rifles, standard issue, that happened to have gone missing from Fort Dix, their absence from inventory unlikely to be detected. They're for my friends in Ireland, friends who badly need them."

I stared at my old pal. "Friends?"

"Actually, not. They are more than friends. They are my brothers-in- arms. I am sort of an officer in the intelligence service of the Irish Republican Army."

"An officer in The IRA. You? It's not a terrorist organization? The newspapers say so."

"So say the English, too. But I believe that the English called George Washington a terrorist. Truly, Al, we're patriots. We fight to rid our land of an oppressor."

"But Ireland has been free for years."

"Al, they haven't left! They're in charge up north. They still have their grip. The worst of them have simply moved to where there's more money to be taken from our hides, where the labor is cheaper, where the bloody Crown still rules everything, where they still run the cops and the courts, where the Protestants are given six votes for every Catholic vote. They maintain an army of occupation. Belfast, man! They have no right to it. We, the IRA, we are making sure they leave Ireland, all of Ireland, once and for all."

"Oh."

What else could I say? For myself, the distinction between the Christian Irish Catholics and the Christian Irish Protestants, who look exactly the same and speak the same language, seems very small. Truthfully, the newspaper reports of the different treaties, the factions, the uprisings, were hard to decipher. It seemed never to end. Or, more precisely, it seemed always to be ending. I would read an announcement that it was over, like when the Irish Free State was founded in 1921, and the next thing I'd see was a report of another round of attacks and marches and arrests and so on. That sort of thing has been going on since before the Great War.

If my friend Mike says his kind of Irish are being treated badly by the other kind of Irish, it's good enough for me. "But what about Seamus? Why did the man running the Wheel of Fortune shoot him?"

I saw something different in Michael as he considered my question. He said, "If I tell ya, somebody may have to shoot ya."

"I've already figured that out," I said. "I've got the most powerful cop in the country gunning for me. Somebody worse? The IRA? You?"

Mike closed the top of the paraffin stove and filled our tin cups with hot coffee.

I said, "So? All of these Irishmen on the pier, they're all illegal. So what?"

"They're not just illegal," Mike said. "They are wanted men. Me too. We have families at risk back home. Livin' with all of that, and keepin' our heads, that's hard enough. Outsiders like you are the last thing we need. We've got enough to deal with."

151

I said, "But you owe me a straight answer. That's
what friends are. I'm up to my eyeballs in your mess and
I have no idea what's going on. I need to know it. I'm as
desperate as you and your gang. Please. Tell me everything."

He blew on the coffee and took a sip. He looked me
in the eye, held my gaze, and began his tale.

"Almost everybody who works on the midway at *Steel
Pier* also works, sort of, for me. Well, I don't actually
pay them, but I got every last one of them his job. They
are fellows we helped to get away before the fuckin'
Royal Irish Constabulary got them into their torture
chambers. We bring them over here on the same ships as
carry the booze. Hamid loves the arrangement: no union,
no labor troubles, low salaries. Any problems, he talks to
me. Most of the lads move on to family in other cities
after a month or two. But the work on the pier doesn't
require real skills, so Hamid has no problems about the
turnover."

"The shooting, Mike. Your man almost killed Seamus!'

"Yeah, that." He swallowed some coffee. "Seamus
has been my lieutenant for over a year, a very good man.
The man who shot him is named Fergus O'Brien. He's
one of the few that I've paid well to keep on the pier for
more than a couple of months. He's actually been there
longer than anyone. Why? Because Fergus's brother is
also one of ours, and he's a staff sergeant with the Quar-

termaster at Fort Dix here in New Jersey. Our Sergeant O'Brien, Fergus's brother, fiddles the books at Fort Dix so that what leaves on the occasional, special truck is removed from the inventory. The driver is also one of our men. We get rifles and Tommy guns.

"That morning, when I came onto the pier with you, Seamus had just come back from counting the cases in *Sweet Emma*'s hold. There were twenty five cases of rifles in this hold, same as there are right now. Seamus had paid Fergus $7,500 for a hundred rifles, four to a case, just like we'll be offloading tonight."

Mike took a *Pall Mall* pack from his shirt pocket and offered me one. We both lit up. Mike continued, "That morning, when you and me arrived at the pier, I agreed to meet Seamus at The Whip ride, where I was planning to talk to a new man and go over the rules. It took Seamus some while to get someone to replace him at the front turnstiles. When he was free, I'd just finished talking to the new man, is when he found me."

Mike shook his head ruefully. "Part of this is that Seamus doesn't the least bit care for Fergus. He knows the man to be a drunk and a petty thief who beats on his women and don't take care of his children. So, he starts right in saying that Fergus has stolen $750 from us, that there's only three rifles in ten of the crates in *Sweet Emma*'s hold. Seamus opened every last one and found ten crates that were a rifle short. I tried to settle him down. 'I'm sure there's a good explanation for it,' I said.

153

"Fergus plays dumb. He has to lie because he's aware of the consequences of stealing from us. So he goes on denying it until you came over to join the conversation. You created just enough of a distraction for the thieving bastard to pull his pistol and get away."

Captain Jack DeWease emerged from the shadows of the alley with two young men. I recognized one of them as William, Mr. Pace's chauffeur. The three came aboard and readied the boat: the section of rail that had been re-moved to allow access from the dock was reattached; the tools and parts were thrown into a box; hatches were closed. DeWease, the elder, went into the wheelhouse and closed the door behind him. I heard a starter motor whine. When the diesel engine caught, a cloud of black smoke belched from a tall stack. The pitch of the engine changed when the propeller was engaged. Jack DeWease slid open a window of the wheelhouse and called out, "Cast off!" The boys slipped the lines and pushed us away from the dock.

Sweet Emma ran slowly out of the short canal toward a green cone-buoy. We turned right around the buoy, into the calm waters of the Absecon Inlet. DeWease opened the throttle a bit and the boat surged east, toward the mouth of the Inlet. To our right, groins of squared black rocks, spaced about a hundred yards apart, jutted into the water from the shadow of the boardwalk. We surged past a red buoy, a gong inside sounding a basso clang in rhythm with the waves. After the last of the groins, we travelled in parallel to the jetty protecting the broad, sandy tip of Absecon Island. Heavy waves were breaking against the rocks and through the girders of a tower at the end of the jetty at the mouth of the Inlet, the entrance to the Atlantic Ocean. A shielded light rotated atop the tower, a beacon for sailors returning in the dark of night.

Smugglers

It was cold on deck, the sun about to set, low on the horizon. Mike went below. I stayed, watching the jetty light turn to a pinpoint behind us. Even though I had only a few hours sleep the night before, despite the fact that I had spent the morning and the afternoon on the run, even though I had worked on the pier for much of the day, I was not tired. In fact, I was excited. I enjoyed the feeling that I didn't know what was going to happen next. I liked the fact that I was on a small boat on a dark, rolling sea.

There had been times, usually when I awakened too early to open the studio, and I lay in the darkness before the dawn, that I had thought of getting dressed and hopping a train to anywhere. I suppose a lot of men, tired of the struggles, have such thoughts. Mine are brief; I would not want to live without Ida and the girls.

As a bachelor in New York, I had found friends in Bowery taverns. Looking back, I realize that I used to be most comfortable with Bohemians, rootless men. I enjoyed spending time with fellows who had done things in Africa and in South American jungles that I longed to do myself. They were painters, prize fighters, actors, and musicians from all over the world and from all over America. One fellow had climbed the Matterhorn.

Another man, a Frenchman, became an especially good friend. He made a living traveling the world, buying gemstones in remote villages from people who were always a threat to murder him or to rob him. He loved to tell me about the tight places from which he had escaped and to show me the rubies and emeralds that he'd brought back. I had been a week away from boarding a freighter with him that was going to take us, partners in the gem business, through the Panama Canal to Indonesia. I had bought the ticket. Then I met Ida.

My neighbors on Chester Avenue, other shopkeepers like myself – the butcher, the haberdasher, the druggist – probably dislike me. They have long since stopped inviting me to their lunches and card games. I suppose they think I am unfriendly.

Ida used to be disappointed that I was not more sociable, that I was so strongly inclined to turn down invitations, that I preferred my magazines and books to dinners with the neighbors. I weary quickly. But I enjoy the company of Michael Finnerty and Sam Brodsky, men others call rogues. That evening as I stood on *Sweet Emma's* cold deck, I felt that I was prepared for whatever came next. Maybe I'm a bit of a rogue myself.

I finally went below. I learned that the other deck-hand's name was Porky. He kept a pipe clamped be-

tween his teeth and was quite thin. Mike slid the bolt on a
locker and took out a deck of cards and a cribbage board.
A kerosene lamp swung above the table where we played
cards, pegging points on the board, a familiar pastime for
both us, one we had often enjoyed back on Chester Avenue. I tired after a couple of games and let Porky take
over my hand.

I was dozing in one of the bunks when Billy came
down and announced, "We see their light. Time to get
ready."

"Do you think there's a coat or a sweater lying
around?" I asked Billy.

"No," he said. Neither Billy nor his father had looked
me in the eye, both ignoring me in a deliberate way.

"Let's have a look," Mike said. He slid the bolt on a
tall locker crammed with Wellington boots and assorted
foul-weather gear. He removed a dark jacket and tossed it
my way. His tightlipped smile said that he understood
that the men were going out of their way to insult me. He
shook his head slightly, a signal that I was not to make
an issue of it.

A large engine started up, and a bright light shone
through the hatchway onto the ladder; Sweet Emma had a
generator. I followed Billy and Mike to the deck where
arc lights mounted on a pole behind the wheelhouse cast
a harsh, hissing light onto the deck, bleaching the color
from everything. I felt momentarily detached from my

body, as if I were in the darkroom, inspecting a negative that was lit from below on the glass of the contact printer.

A freighter loomed ahead, lit by a pale half-moon. Jack DeWease throttled back the engine, slowing our approach to a standstill. I watched a handful of busy men at the rail of the freighter near a winch and derrick. Soon, a floating dock was lowered over the rail. It was a large, wooden pallet attached to oil drums with two truck tires, bumpers, lashed onto each of the four sides. DeWease pushed his boat forward, timing it so that we came alongside the floating dock, and reversed the engine.

Porky pulled the dock toward us with a gaff on a long pole. DeWease, inside the wheel house, disengaged the propeller

Billy, holding the free ends of the ropes, jumped onto the dock and quickly twisted the lines around cleats on the two near corners of the dock. Porky joined Billy and helped him tie the other corners of the dock to large rings welded onto the freighter's side.

The bumpers scraped against the wooden hull of our boat and the steel hull of the freighter, groaning with the rise and fall of the calm sea. The winch's motor whined, drawing my attention above my head, to an empty cargo net made of heavy rope that was being lowered to the floating dock. As soon as it touched, Porky detached it from the hook and spread it wide.

I watched them offload the rifles. Billy hopped back onto Sweet Emma and lifted a large hatch cover, dragged it across the deck and leaned it against the rail. He climbed down a steep ladder into the hold. In a minute, I saw the end of a wooden case with a rope handle get pushed upward until it tilted onto the deck. Mike had been waiting for it. He grabbed the handle and pulled the heavy case over the boards to the rail. I saw the five pointed star and block-lettered, "U.S. Army " stenciled in a deep blue stain along the raw wood side of the case.

Mike pulled a second case onto the deck. Porky dragged it across to the rail near the freighter. I watched the process, fighting an urge to help. Instead, I kept my hands in my pockets and leaned my back against a mast to watch. Yes, I was composing photographs in my head. But it wasn't only the deep shadows and geometric shapes that etched the scene into my memory; it was the nature of what the men were doing - I was watching them break the laws of Britain and America. What in hell was "The Law " to those men? To me?

To Mike, British and American laws were hazards of war, like mines on a battlefield. What allowed him to feel that he was in the right, his shield of virtue, was a conviction that he was fighting to set his countrymen free. The law was of no matter by comparison.

Nucky thought of the laws as tools. He believed that he had the right to ignore certain laws, or certain people, like Hoover, if they interfered with people earning a living in his orderly community. Laws were just ways to make adjustments to society's machine: the voters, the cops, the judges, the elected officials, and the bureaucrats. Nucky saw himself as the benevolent engineer who kept everything running smoothly.

Sam was of the Robin Hood school; laws were enacted by an elite group to manage society for its own, narrow benefit. He, born poor, had an obligation to take from them. He would have thought less of himself, that he was lacking in the virtue of competence, had he not taken advantage of the hypocrites who happened to be in charge. It was not Sam's fault that the laws were stupid and hypocritical; it was entirely the fault of the stupid hypocrites who ran things in America, people like J. Edgar Hoover.

Hoover, I guessed, believed he was perfecting America, ridding it of those who did not believe in achieving the perfect society from sea to shining sea. Lawbreakers were evil because they were in opposition to America's holy purpose. Edgar Hoover was the High Priest in the sacred order called "Federal Government."

When there were twelve cases by the rail, Billy emerged from the hold and joined Mike and Porky in building a neat stack of American rifles on the cargo net. Mike called to the freighter to lower the hook. As soon as the cargo net and its contents started upward, the men returned to Sweet Emma, went to the hold and started building the next stack.

To Ida, the issue was always personal. It was *not* about right, wrong, legal or illegal; it was about good people and bad people. I had learned to trust her instincts. Often, she took an instant dislike to someone, and most of the time, after awhile, I would find out that her judgment had been spot-on. I recalled that Ida's first question had been about whether Hoover was, or was not, a good man. If he was, then *I* would have been in the wrong, because I would have damaged a good person.

What about me? As I watched the men around me break laws, I realized that I had not been honest with my-self. Watching the gun runners and the rum runners, I realized that I was glad to have been discovered, that I was ashamed of what I had been doing in the blind. Whether legal or not, observing people when they don't know they're being watched or eavesdropping when they don't know they are being overheard is repugnant. We have an inalienable right to our secrets, to keep fragments of ourselves to ourselves.

But my opinion doesn't matter to anyone but me. I don't think there should be a law against people drinking or gambling, either. It is the opinions of people like Hoover and Nucky that actually matter, whether legal or not, right or wrong. Hoover, apparently, had the right to listen to Nucky's private telephone conversations. He would

163

claim, I guessed, that he was doing so for the betterment of holy America, that eavesdropping was a means justified by an end.

The pile of wood boxes rose up to the freighter.

There was something primitive about the way Hoover and Johnson were behaving. An image came to mind, of Nucky and Edgar as stallions confronting each other on the perimeter of a herd, rearing and screaming, each concerned about nothing more than the right to rule. The Johnsons and the Hoovers of the world use laws to keep their power, to wield their power, to diminish the power of their rivals. They want more influence for themselves, less for their rivals. It's not about justice or fairness, right, wrong or the greater good for such people. It's about satisfying an overwhelming, personal compulsion to be in command, to answer to no one else, to be the one and only one with power. These are the men who would be kings, or czars, or directors.

The second net full of rifles was rising beside the freighter. I walked to the hold and looked down — empty. Mike, Billy, and I lit cigarettes. Porky knocked his pipe bowl empty, refilled it from an oilskin pouch, struck a match into flame, and puffed patches of smoke into the wind. We watched as a man was lowered from the freighter, a foot in the hook and a hand on the rope.

"Dennis!" exclaimed Mike, jumping onto the dock and embracing the man. For a few minutes, they con-

versed in tones too quiet for me to hear. Mike handed
Dennis an envelope, Dennis reached inside his coat and
pulled out a fat envelope and handed it to Mike. Both
men opened the packets and scanned the sheaves of paper. The man called Dennis put his foot into the hook and
hollered up to be lifted.

Mike watched the derrick above him, even after Dennis had been swung out of our sight. A minute later, a
small man holding a suitcase in one hand and the rope
with the other, began the descent to the dock. When he
landed, Mike extended a hand to help the guy board
Sweet Emma.

He was a fair-skinned young man, a boy really, with
tendrils of hair curling out from the edges of a knit cap.
The newcomer looked at the three of us and said, "Got a
fag, anyone?"

We stared at him.

"A fag," he said. "A cigarette. Will one of yez be kind
enough to be offerin' me a cigarette?" It took a moment
to make out what he was saying through the lilting
rhythm and twisted vowels of his accent. Then I got it
and offered him one from my pack.

The winch motor whined from above. A cube-shaped
bundle slowly descended to the floating dock. Porky settled it down and removed the hook. He began transferring
boxes of *Simmons Plymouth Gin* to the rail. Billy, wait-

ing, carried them across the deck and set them down next to the hold.

"Mike," I said, "Let me help."

"Why not? Why don't you and me carry these cases to the hold and let Billy stow them? Is that alright with you, Billy?" Mike said.

Billy glanced at me and said, "Sure. Save some time." He climbed into the hold. His father was in the wheel-house still, minding the idling engine.

Mike said, "I'll be up to lend a hand as soon as I get our new arrival here settled below."

"Let me finish me fag, first. Why canno' I stay here, anyways?" protested the boy.

"No reason," said Mike. "Suit yourself."

The cargo net dropped four more loads onto the float-ing dock. Dennis, grasping the rope, was balanced atop the final pile. He slid down and managed to get both feet onto the dock; I saw that one of his legs did not bend at the knee.

Even miles from land, on the heaving deck of a tiny fishing boat on a moonlit night, business is business, whether legal or not. Mike finished checking the cargo, penciling tic marks on the paperwork, and climbed up onto the deck. Dennis thumped across to join him. The hissing arc lights, powered by the roaring generator, cast black shadows.

Michael and Dennis exchange papers, embraced, patted each other heartily on the back. Dennis climbed awkwardly over the rail and onto the dock. With his good foot in the hook, he yelled to be hoisted, and with a final wave to his friend, ascended to the freighter.

When the hook was dropped for the last time, Billy and Porky untied the floating dock and hopped onto the *Sweet Emma*. Mike hollered up for the men on the larger ship to hoist the contraption up. DeWease powered his boat in a turn away when the thing was barely clear of the waves. It was moments later that I learned how the man in the wheelhouse really felt about me — he didn't like me.

As I was going across the deck, passing the wheelhouse window, intending to go down to the crew quarters, DeWease pulled the switch on the generator. Blinded, disoriented by the sudden silence on a tilting deck, I fell to my knees and waited for my vision to return. I imagined the captain in the wheelhouse. Surely, he'd seen me, away from any handhold, when he shut off the generator. Yet, he had not warned me. I sensed that he was watching my clumsy effort to keep my balance, perhaps with a smile on his face.

Eventually, my vision returned, allowing me to stand and make my way around the deck without danger of falling overboard. At the stern rail, I watched the silvery wake stream behind us. Still angry, I went along the rail to the prow where I tried, unsuccessfully, to discern the glow of Atlantic City below the starry horizon. With the wind in my face, I stared ahead until my anger cooled. Eventually, I left the deck and went below to rest.

By the lantern's feeble glow, I saw that Billy, Porky, and Mike each occupied a bunk. The red-haired, Irish wetback lay sleeping on a blanket on the floor. Apparently, Mike had reserved a mattress for me. I climbed up to the fourth bunk and fell asleep.

I dreamt of the hotel fire escape. There were no doorways. The tower was deep and dark and endless. I was stumbling, falling, going faster and faster. There was no way out; I could not stop.

Dance Floor

We returned to the Rhode Island Avenue Canal at daybreak. DeWease cut the engine to dead slow as he entered the narrow passage of the canal after making the turn at the green buoy. After a night at open throttle, the sudden quiet of the diesel came as a relief. Ahead, the surface of the canal was like a mirror. DeWease maneuvered Sweet Emma into its berth with ease, causing a wake that set two trawlers docked at the wharf to rise and fall in their moorings.

Ida, surprisingly, was waiting on the wharf. After Porky removed the rail, I jumped off the boat, dropped the valise and plunged into her arms. I inhaled the scent of her hair. She held me with all her strength. In the comfort of her embrace, the anxiety that had been driving me since yesterday morning ebbed like a receding tide. I stepped back for a better view of the face I'd happily slept beside for twenty years.

"Hello, sailor," she said.

"It's a little early for you, isn't it?"

"Who else was going to tell you to come home? J. Edgar Hoover?"

She turned to Mike who was stepping onto the dock with the wetback. "And you," said my wife, "Some care you take of my Albert! On this kind of a boat you take him?! What's the matter with you? "

"I am so terribly sorry, my dear lady," he said. " 'Tis, indeed, an awful boat. But look at the man. He's fit as a fiddle, none the worse for the wear of a black night on the bounding main."

She regarded me with a squint, "He needs a shave. And a bath. And you, yourself, Mr. Finnerty, you're not so spiffy, either."

Mike laughed. "Let me introduce you to our new friend. This here is Mr. Johnny Dwyer, who at this very moment, is as green a greenhorn as ever was. Say hello to Ida Rubin."

The young man pulled the knit cap from his head, stuffed it into the pocket of his coat and ran his fingers through a mop of red hair. He managed a brief, faint smile. "A pleasure," he said.

"Welcome to America," said Ida.

"We'd best get out of their way," said Mike, referring to a pair of teamsters who had appeared with a hand truck. Porky and Billy had positioned a ramp on either side of the rail to make it easier to roll the cargo onto the dock from Sweet Emma's hold. Jack DeWease, standing by the wheelhouse, regarded the sudden crowd on the dock. I did not like the way he was looking at Ida.

"Not quite yet," I said.

Mike grabbed my arm, trying to stop me, as I strode to the ramp. Pulling away, I walked onto *Sweet Emma's* deck toward DeWease, Mike following.

"You need to apologize," I said. "You saw me walking across the deck when you killed the lights. You knew I'd be blinded. You didn't warn me. What the hell is the matter with you?"

The Captain finally looked me in the eye. "I don't apologize to nobody on my own boat, especially to no Jewboy. Get the fuck off, or I'll throw you off."

I raised my fists.

DeWease smiled, the first I'd seen on his weathered face. As he was swinging a roundhouse right toward the side of my head, a punch that I had somehow been expecting since I first saw the man, I popped him with a left jab and ducked under his big fist. I saw blood from his nose spurt bright onto the bristles of his upper lip as he stumbled backward. He regained his balance and rushed me. I stepped aside and tripped him as he passed. As he was falling forward, I drove my right fist deep into his side, just below the ribs.

When he got up, confused about why he had been on his face on the deck, I could see that he wasn't yet feeling the pain from my kidney punch; he'd likely see blood the next time he pissed. He came toward me, posing with his fists pointing up like he was a boxer on a fight poster.

171

The longer it lasted, the harder it would be for me to get off the boat. From a crouch, I threw a left cross toward his right ear. When he raised his hand to protect himself, I hit him in the pit of his stomach with my right fist so hard that I almost felt his spine. That did it. He was on his hands and knees, struggling to catch a breath, no doubt worried whether he'd ever breathe again.

Mike managed to get himself between me and Billy. The younger DeWease, who saw his duty as fighting with me, was several inches taller than his father but not as heavily muscled. He tried to get at me by pushing Mike aside. Mike, who was as big as the younger man and a lot more experienced, pulled Billy off balance and sent him stumbling toward the rail.

"That's enough," said Mike. "Albert, would you get yourself off the damned boat, please?" He stood in front of Billy, who made a less forceful attempt to get past Mike. I walked down the ramp onto the dock. Standing next to my wife, I saw that the Captain was still on his hands and knees.

"Sorry," I said to Ida. I grabbed the valise and I took my wife's hand. I led her up the short alley toward the street. "The man's an anti-Semite. Did you hear what he said to me?"

"I heard."

"I had no choice."

"You did so."

172

"Okay, I had a choice. I chose to punch him."

"A good thing, too."

Mike and Johnny Dwyer followed us up the alley. We stood on the sidewalk, across from Mike's *Reo*. He said, "Shall I drive you home?"

"It's just up the street," I said. "I will enjoy the feel of solid ground."

"Ida," said Mike, "I don't think it's safe for Al at your house. He should be finding a place to lay low for awhile."

"We think it's safe," she said.

"We? What we?"

"Sam and I. And Nucky."

Mike regarded her for a long moment. "And how did you come to be having a conversation with the likes of Nucky Johnson?"

"As we were dancing. At the Ball."

"You danced with Nucky Johnson at the Convention Hall Ball?"

"Twice. He's quite the foxtrot *maven*, let me tell you. Of course, I danced with Sam, too. He's not so good. Anne says she's going to enroll them in a dance class."

"Do you care to tell me what they said? I have an interest, you know," said Mike.

Ida came to Mike, grabbed his arm, raised up on her toes and kissed him on the cheek. "I'm sure they will tell you all about it. Thanks for taking care of Al. You're a good friend. Now I've got to get him home and clean him up."

"Can I stop by later?" he asked.

"Any time," she said, and we walked up the street toward 113 North Rhode Island Avenue. We climbed the stairs to the porch and entered quietly through the front door so as not to disturb Helen and Pauline, still asleep in their separate bedrooms. The stairs creaked. In our sparsely furnished bedroom , I whispered, "Do I really need a bath?"

Ida whispered back, "You really do. But I think you should wait awhile."

"You do?"

"I really do," she said.

And we made love.

§

At the kitchen table, after a short nap and a hot bath, as we drank coffee, Ida told me what had transpired at the Ball. "We took a taxi from here to the Convention Hall, since you weren't around to drive us."

"Sorry. It couldn't be helped. I told Mike that I didn't want to go on that boat. We passed right by the house. I told him to stop, but he wouldn't do it."

"A likely story," she planted a kiss on the top of my head. Then she planted a punch on my arm.

"Okay," I said. "Just tell me about Nucky and Sam. And leave out what good dancers they are, please."

Ida had spent weeks making the dresses with Helen and Pauline. It had been hard work for her, as much to keep the girls from losing their tempers over the repeated fittings as to keep their spirits up as they looked at themselves in the long mirror of the sewing room. More than once, from the living room, where I read and listened to the radio in the evenings, I heard outbursts of exasperation interspersed with the sweet lilt of Ida's reason.

Helen, seventeen, had her mother make a dress out of dark blue velvet that complimented her olive complexion. The dress pattern flattened her front, she thought, de-emphasizing her ample bosom. She had not gotten used to men staring at her.

Honey-blonde, fair-skinned, fifteen-year old Pauline had chosen a bright pink satin fabric. Apparently, she liked the staring.

Ida, with the same coloring as Pauline, made herself a dress that almost matched the color of her light brown hair. The hemlines were just below the knees. "Very nice," I'd say, as they came into the living room and twirled. "You are beautiful," I said to each one.

The girls had not panicked when I disappeared from the *Steel Pier*. Gabriel had so much darkroom work that he hadn't emerged to face the public even once; he barely noticed that I was gone. Ida had kept them all calm, reassuring them that everything was going to be all right, that they had to take turns dealing with the continuous line of

175

customers waiting for their pictures while the other worked at the cash register. Ida stayed behind the camera and told people to smile. She told the girls that they didn't need me and the *De Soto*... that they would take a taxi to the Ball... that Gabriel would provide escort... that everything was going to be fine.

"What else could I do?" said Ida, stirring sugar into her coffee.

The invitation to the Ball had said that the dancing was to begin at 8 o'clock. Ida closed up Memories at 5 o'clock and they walked the mile home, allowing barely enough time to eat and primp. Ida phoned for a taxi, timing it to pick up Gabriel and for them to make an entrance at nine. In any event, they hadn't gotten onto the dance floor until after nine thirty, because there had been such a long line of taxis and limousines dropping people off.

"You missed it, Al. What a place! Do you remember when we went to look at St Patrick's Cathedral in New York? How huge it is? Well, I think the Convention Hall is bigger than that. And all these people who got invited, there must have been a thousand people there, they took up just a tiny little space on a dance floor in the middle of the whole hall. And guess who they had playing?"

She waited. I shrugged.

"Guy Lombardo!"

Ida had kept a motherly eye on her pretty daughters, both of whom were in demand as dance partners for the many single men. "They both had a terrific time! I'm afraid our Helen has two left feet," she said. "Gabriel, I'm afraid, did not have much fun. He sort of disappeared. Every time I saw him, he would give a little wave and take a sip from a cup of punch. Later, he told me that he did not know how to dance. Apparently, it's not something they teach at *gymnasium*. But that Nucky! What a smoothie! What a dancer. And *so* handsome. Al, I want us to get you one of those tuxedoes."

I sipped my coffee, sympathizing with Gabriel.

Sam had been there with his fiancée, Anne Adler. He had been happy that his cousin decided to come to the Ball in spite of my absence. Sam told her that it was he who suggested that Mike take me onto the *Sweet Emma*, one of his boats, until the fuss died down. He reassured her that Mike would keep me safe. It was a calm night, he told her, the boat went out on nights like it all the time. He told her where the boat docked and about when he expected it to return.

"Sam says that Hoover put two and two together right away. He guessed that you were the man in 1202, the photographer, the one married to Sam's cousin. But Nucky says we shouldn't worry."

Sam said that Nucky wanted to meet her, that he had something to tell her. Her cousin escorted her onto the

177

dance floor where he introduced her to Nucky. Nucky left his partner, a woman wearing a loose fitting, slinky. Ida thought the woman was probably a showgirl. And off she had danced with Nucky

Settled at the kitchen table, Ida tried to imitate Nucky's polished accent, "My dear Mrs. Rubin, I've heard so much about you. Shall we dance?"

Ida said, "What a smoothie! But I don't think the man was dazzled by my beauty; he just wanted to send you some messages."

"The hell with him. I'm dazzled," I said, remembering what had so wonderfully transpired upstairs a short while before.

"Nucky said that he would appreciate it if you pay him a visit as soon as you can."

"I expected that," I said. "When I talked to Louie, yesterday, after I ran from the hotel, he told me that Nucky would want to talk to me."

Nucky had tried to reassure Ida that her husband was not in trouble. According to the Czar, Hoover couldn't prove that I broke federal laws, so there was nothing for him to enforce. And I had not broken local laws, either. The local courts would not be issuing Hoover any warrants. The Director of the Investigations Bureau had already asked a judge, who happened to have been a friend of Nucky's, no surprise there, and the judge refused him. The Atlantic City police would be polite to Hoover, but no more. "So, if Hoover's people keep talking to you, you shouldn't be intimidated. Nucky says so! Do you get it, Al? You're safe. The law's on our side. At least in Atlantic City."

I doubted that, but said, "That's good news."

After her second dance with Nucky, she went to stand with Anne and Sam. Sam offered a car and driver to Ida and the girls for a ride home. Sam and Anne would go back to the penthouse atop the Ritz Carlton, just a block away.

I raised an eyebrow at this because their wedding was still a couple of weeks off. Ida said, "Well what do you think? They're as good as married. Besides, it's none of our business. Anyway, I was grateful for the ride. Otherwise, we would probably have stood in line for a taxi for an hour. My shoes were killing me. It was very nice of Sam to offer."

That had been when Sam pointed Hoover out to Ida. This was surprising news to me; if ever I had seen a man in a huff, it had been J. Edgar Hoover with his fists on the front desk of the Ritz Carlton Hotel. I had thought surely he would have left town in said huff.

"So he's still in Suite 1200?" I asked.

Not so. According to Sam, he checked out and had his bags taken over to the *Marlborough-Blenheim Hotel*.

"I must say, J. Edgar Hoover is impressive. He carries himself like he's royalty," Ida said. "But he was so odd.

179

Scary. He didn't take his eyes off Nucky the whole night. Whenever I'd look, he was giving Nucky this 'look.' If looks could kill, if you know what I mean. All night, he stood there, next to a tall man and the Senator from New Jersey. Whenever I looked, he was just glaring at Nucky.

"Nucky ignored him. Then the Senator walks over to Nucky and brings him back to Hoover and introduces the two of them. I watched," said Ida. "Hoover didn't say anything when they were introduced; he just kept on giving Nucky that look. Nucky paid him no mind. After a couple of minutes, Nucky found somebody else to dance with."

"The tall man was probably Clement Talbot," I said. "The same man who was with him in the hotel."

"Tell me about the pictures," said my wife. "Were they really naughty? How naughty? Was it disgusting? You know, Hoover didn't dance once the whole night. I didn't even see him talking to a woman."

"Please, I don't want to talk about it. It's not for you to know. Ladies should not be interested in such things," I said.

"Spoil sport," said my wife.

"Daddy!" said Helen as she entered the kitchen. "You're home!"

Mistaken Assumption

Late in the morning, the four of us walked to the pier, because I had left the *De Soto* overnight in the parking lot. The attendant said it was good that I finally showed up, as he was about to have it towed away. I thanked him for his patience, paid for the day before, and *schmeared* him twenty-five cents.

Gabriel had been waiting. "I didn't know what time to be here. I didn't want to be late," he said.

There were not many people on the pier. It was early on a warm, sunny day, the kind of day that people would prefer to spend on the beach, not an amusement pier.

We'd only had *Memories* opened up for a couple of minutes when Clement Talbot, wearing a white Panama with a red band, walked up to the counter. He glanced toward my family, leaned toward me and quietly said, "Do you know who I am?"

I thought it over and said, "You look familiar."

We stared at each other. Eventually he said, "My name is Clement Talbot." I waited, expecting him to say that he is an agent of the Justice Department. He did not.

"How do you do. My name is Albert Rubin. What's your business, Mr. Talbot?"

181

"Listen, Rubin, we need to talk. Can you come with me for a few minutes?"

I thought it over. "You can see that we are busy here. Please, what's your business?"

He leaned all the way forward and whispered, "This is about the pictures, God damn it! The pictures you took in the hotel yesterday morning."

I was careful to show nothing as I pondered how I should respond to the man. I stepped around the counter. "Ida," I said in a loud voice, "Do you see that bench over there next to the cotton candy stall? Mr. Talbot and I are going to talk for a few minutes over there. Is that okay by you, Mr. Talbot?"

Ida looked at Talbot, then at me. "Everything will be fine," she said. "Go. Take care of business." Pauline and Helen, hearing their mother's odd tone of voice, inspected Talbot, who had not stopped staring, glowering, at me.

Steel Pier is big enough to have different neighborhoods. My stall was the last establishment in the high-rent district, under the roof that protects the theatres and permanent exhibit areas. The cotton candy stall was safely in the open, bathed in the sunshine of the first day of June, on the stretch of midway that leads to the water circus and the section of pipe railing where fishing is allowed.

"What can I do for you, Mr. Talbot? I have some pictures, you say?"

"Wise guy!" he flared, reddening. "Just knock it off. You are not cute. I *know* that you were in Room 1202 of the *Ritz Carlton* the night before last. I *know* you took a camera with you when you left. I have hotel niggers who describe you down to your mustache and your accent. So, I know it was you! We developed what was in the other camera, so we know you doctored the film for low light."

If I had been Hoover and Talbot, I would have assumed that a camera was missing because I would have found one in the living room and an identical setup, without a camera, in the bedroom. Also, there were two leather carrying cases and two *Rolleiflex* manuals in the equipment box. They didn't know what was on the film in the missing camera; they only knew what had happened, what had transpired in Suite 1200 between the time they returned from the *Entertainers Club* and the time that Pierre had knocked on their door.

"I want the negatives. I want the prints. Now!" he said, his voice rising. "I promise that you will regret the day you were born unless you hand them over to me."

"I have no pictures."

Apparently, he had not heard what I said. "You will be subpoenaed for wearing shoes. We will find reasons to depose you so that you will spend every damned day for the rest of your life answering questions under oath. We will bring indictments against you for crimes that you did not know existed. I want those pictures."

I didn't think Hoover could have behaved otherwise – he couldn't help himself. I had only observed him for one night, but I did form a strong impression; J. Edgar Hoover was a person who must have control. He'd stayed in town to take charge of the situation and force events, to make things come out a way he chose to have them. He probably felt as if he had no choice.

The fact that it was Talbot, not Dixon or Whitehead or any of their agents, suggested to me that they wanted to deal with the problem in a way that did not involve the Bureau. The likes of Whitehead and Dixon, their own investigators, might have started rumors within the Investigations Bureau. That would not have been good for Hoover. No, he and Talbot had come to the conclusion that they had no option but to solve the problem of Al Rubin themselves.

"*I* have no pictures," I repeated, slowly.

He stared at me. "Do you mean somebody else has them?"

"I am guessing that these are embarrassing photographs? Believe me, if I had them, I would be happy to give them to you."

He took a deep breath and looked to the sky, perhaps hoping for divine guidance.

"Do you know Mr. Enoch Johnson?" I asked.

Talbot answered quickly, "I have heard of the man. He's the boss of the local machine. He runs the *Ritz Carl-*

ton. He knew about the cameras in 1202, didn't he? He had to."

"Probably. After all, it is his hotel. I am pleased to say that Mr. Johnson is a business associate of mine."

"And? He has them?"

"Mr. Nucky Johnson is very well connected with all of the businessmen in Atlantic City, perhaps he can find out whether these photographs are available. Shall I ask him to do that for you?"

What a state Edgar must have been in! He had questioned the people who helped me set up the blind. They told him there had been two cameras. Something must have happened in the bedroom that he believed was in the other *Rolleiflex*.

He had gone to the Ball with the Senator and stood, waiting, through the whole long evening, enduring Guy Lombardo and *The Pennsylvanians*, seething with anger, inviting someone to approach. No one had. Ida's story suggested that he asked the Senator to make an introduction to Nucky. How frustrated he must have been that Nucky played the innocent.

Talbot replied, "You will speak to Johnson about this? What will you tell him?"

"What would you like me to tell him?"

He stiffened and looked down at me. "You little ....!" he said. "For Christ's sake, stop the games. There is nothing funny about any of this. You know who I am. You know what I want. Just tell Johnson that we are ready to negotiate. Can you do that?"

I stood and looked him in the eye. "Mr. Talbot," I said. "I can see that you are upset. No doubt, you have your reasons. I will convey your message to Mr. Johnson."

"How soon can you talk to him."

"Soon. Maybe today. I will bring this matter to his attention."

Talbot said, "Make sure it's today. This will be resolved soon or, I promise you, forces will be unleashed that you cannot imagine. It is Friday." He looked at his wrist watch. "It is eleven o'clock in the morning. My associate and I are leaving town on Sunday afternoon. We want this matter settled before we leave."

"How can I get in touch with you?"

"We're... I'm at the *Marlborough-Blenheim*. Just call the operator and ask for me." He turned on his heel and left without offering to shake hands. I can't say as I blamed him for being rude. I lost sight of his white hat in the shadowed space under the roof.

Ida, I knew, had been watching me and Talbot. When I returned to *Memories,* she said, "That's the man who was with Hoover at the Ball. What did you tell him?"

I smiled and gave her a big hug. "I said I'd stay in touch."

A half hour later, I used the phone booth on the Boardwalk to call the *Ritz*. Louie said that Nucky had been waiting to hear from me. I said I would come by as soon as I got my assistant squared away in the darkroom. He said there was no rush, to come after four o'clock, after Nucky had his breakfast.

Rolling Chair

At four o'clock, I was at the *Ritz Carlton*. Nucky poured coffee into our cups from a silver pot as we sat opposite each other on striped silk sofas in his living room. "I had the privilege of dancing with Mrs. Rubin the other night. She is a beautiful, lovely woman."

"Everybody loves her. What can I say? I'm a lucky man."

"Al, I am beginning to believe that there is more to you than luck. They tell me that you brought Jack DeWease to his knees with one punch. True?"

"Well," I said, "There were three, actually. Lucky shots. Another time, another place, he would probably clean my clock. He's a big, strong fellow."

"And mean. You had best be careful around Jack. I have known him my entire life. We went to the same schoolhouse as children. He can be vicious and calculating. You probably made an enemy."

"Nucky, the man was my enemy before he ever laid eyes on me. He is a Jew hater. He wanted to hurt me from the minute I stepped onto his boat."

"It is *not* his boat, it is Sam's. DeWease captains it so long as Sam chooses to pay him." He took a sip of coffee and set his cup down. "Al, Louie says you overheard Hoover talking about me. What did he say?"

I guess I was paying special attention because I was able to repeat what Talbot and Hoover had said, almost word for word. Nucky listened, shaking his head in wonderment, occasionally interjecting to indicate astonishment or disapproval. When I recounted what they'd said after they returned from dinner at the *Entertainers Club*, he said, "Well that proves it right there."

"Proves what?"

"The *Entertainers Club* is a place for men who like men instead of women. It's a word-of-mouth operation, high class, the kind of place that doesn't advertise – it doesn't even have a sign out front. So, Mr. J. Edgar Hoover knew all about the *Entertainers Club.*"

I finished, summing it up this way, "Hoover doesn't think anyone has the right to ignore him. He thinks you have too much power."

This lit Nucky's fuse. "Me? Too much power? I am telling no secrets, Al, when I say that there is a feeling growing in Washington that it is Edgar Hoover who has too much power. Edgar Hoover already has the reputation of an untouchable, a man beyond reproach. He's a bureaucratic juggernaut, the darling of every appropriations committee he appears before."

"But it's not just that he's efficient and patriotic. There are dozens of dedicated men who have been made "Director" of one agency or another. Most of them are outstanding civil servants. I think there's something else going on with this Hoover that makes him more than a good bureaucrat. You have confirmed it. He spies on people. How did he put it about eavesdropping on my telephone? Tidbits?"

He rose from the couch, went to the big window overlooking the beach and adjusted the cords on the venetian blinds. It was still full daylight. "I have friends in Washington," he said. "I know every Congressman from every Middle Atlantic state. I know the Senators. I have entertained Governors from all over the country in this very room. I am pleased to say that most of these men consider me their friend. I am telling no secrets, Al, when I say that there is a feeling growing in Washington that Edgar Hoover has become, unto himself, The Law. He answers to no party nor to any elected official. Coolidge's Attorney General, Sargent, let him have his head. We'll see what the new Attorney General, Mitchell, does. My guess is nothing.

"Lately, I have heard people saying, 'Watch out for J. Edgar Hoover.' I have seen powerful men clam up and change the subject at the mention of his name. Their behavior tells me that he's collecting 'little tidbits' on elected officials.

"Think about it, Al. I don't care if he is the reincarnation of George Washington and Abraham Lincoln rolled into one, which he definitely is not, it's too much power. One man, who answers to no one, with all of the investigative power of the Justice Department, who collects and files secret information about the members of Congress. Judges too, I'll bet. He has people listening to my telephone conversations, for God's sake! Me! Can you imagine the kind of influence he wields."

"The other night, at the Ball, he gets Wally Edge to introduce us. So, as a favor to Wally, I go along and agree to meet the great J. Edgar Hoover. I was not well pleased, let me tell you. What an odious man!"

He shook his head and breathed a deep sigh. "It's just too bad that they found you out before you could get any pictures. My God, how wonderful it would be to have a few valuable tidbits on J. Edgar Hoover. Too damn bad."

"But, Nucky," I said, "They think that there are pictures."

"But there aren't. The film in the second camera was not exposed, right?"

"That is correct, but ..." I told Nucky about Talbot's visit.

When I was finished, the Czar faced the sea and slid his enormous hands into the pockets of his cream-colored trousers. He twisted to look at me, then looked back out over the beach to the bright horizon. When he turned around, he was smiling.

"Al, you sly dog. You dog! You told Talbot there were no pictures, right?"

"No. I said that *I* had no pictures. I said maybe you, the great Nucky Johnson, could maybe find them for us."

He laughed some more. "And that's the truth, *n'est-ce pas*? Oh, Albert, there is definitely more to you than meets the eye. I don't suppose you have a blind set up in the *Marlborough-Blenheim*, do you?"

"Sorry, Nucky, but my days of secret photography are over. It's just not for me."

Louie came to the archway between the living room and the dining room. "What's funny?" I repeated the story for Louie.

"So," said Nucky, "Maybe it's not over."

"Is Sam still in town?" I asked. "As you say, he's a smart fellow. Maybe not a genius, like you say, but he definitely knows how to make a deal. I think you should ask him if maybe he has ideas."

Nucky said, "Even if he's in New York, I'd beg him to come down for this."

Louie called down to the desk and found out that Sam and Anne still had a lot of their belongings in their suite. Louie left a message saying that Sam was to get in touch with Nucky. "Urgent," said Louie. "Put 'urgent' in the message. And call me the minute he walks into the lobby."

"Albert," said Nucky, "Let me introduce you to the delights of good champagne and fresh-squeezed orange juice, the perfect beverage for a sunny morning."

I didn't mention that it was approaching five o'clock in the afternoon. I said goodbye, anxious to put the *Ritz*

Carlton behind me, to get back to the *Steel Pier* where I had a flourishing business to run.

One of the bellhops, a fellow who'd helped me out when I'd set up the blind, caught up to me on my way through the lobby. "Mr. Rubin, there's somebody who would like to talk to you. Can you wait here a minute, please? He was just outside awhile ago." The bellhop hurried through the revolving door to The Boardwalk and returned immediately. "He's still there."

On The Boardwalk, standing behind an empty rolling chair, was Charles Henderson, the man who told Pierre about the mirrors.

"Please, Mr. Albert," he said, "I needs to talk to you. Will you let me give you a ride?"

"Really, Mr. Henderson, I like to walk."

"Please," he said.

So, I sat myself down. "I'd like to get to the Steel Pier as fast as I can. You can tell me what you have to say on the way."

It was my first ride in a rolling chair and it made me feel silly. The Boardwalk had lanes for those conveyances. If, as you strolled along, you dawdled in one of the lanes, you would hear a Negro man call out from behind you, "Watch the chair! Watch the chair!' The men who did the pushing were all Negroes. The chairs were built by putting car seats into wicker contraptions that had a push bar across the back, a canvas canopy to shade the passengers, and three rubber wheels underneath. For myself, the thought of using another man's muscles to get me from place to place had never been appealing.

Mr. Henderson said, "I been waiting on you, Mr. Albert. Wallace, the bell captain, he promise to tell me when you was going to be around so I could talk to you." He saw a space in the crowd of people walking on the eastbound lane and quickly maneuvered the chair into it. I felt conspicuous, embarrassed that people who saw me would think I was a lazy or stuck-up kind of guy.

Charles hollered, "Watch the chair!" Without turning, the strollers ambled away from the smooth lane of parallel boards.

He spoke to me, "You and me, we work together like men. I didn't want you in no trouble. I am sorry for what happen with Pierre,".

"Okay," I said. "It was pretty bad. Your brother-in-law chased me down the fire escape."

"That's awful. But I couldn't do nothing about it. It was my wife, Iris, who done it. Her brother was eating breakfast with us and he saying about how his boss is staying on the twelfth floor, and Iris say, 'Isn't that where you put in those funny mirrors?' I *try* to shut her up by saying I don't know what she talking about. But she keep at it, saying don't I remember the secret doorway and how I hung one-way mirrors on the twelfth floor. Pierre, he all over it. He pester me. I felt like I can't make my Iris into a liar, so I tells him. I tries to make it sound like nothing, but I guess he think it something. I am really sorry."

"It's all right Mr. Henderson," I said. "I got out in time. Nobody blames you."

"Mr. Louie, he blame me. I think maybe I lose my winter job at the hotel, if he still mad at me. Will you speak to Mr. Louie about me?" he pleaded. "I am a good carpenter."

"I know you are," I said.

The previous Presidential election, 1928, in Philadelphia, where a Republican was always the Mayor and where Republicans had all of the important political jobs, there were a lot of people, mostly Catholics, who voted for the Democrat, Al Smith. But that was not true of Atlantic City which is only sixty miles away. That November, when Herbert Hoover won in New Jersey by a twenty percent margin, he won in Atlantic City with almost ninety per cent of the vote. That was because of the Negroes.

Charles and I had found out that we were both interested in politics as we ate our sandwiches and shared cigarettes during the time we spent building the blind in 1202. He had explained to me that the Negroes vote for Republicans because of Abraham Lincoln, and because, in the Southern states, the Democrats won't let them vote at all. In Atlantic City, it was the other way around. If you were Negro, the white people almost forced you to vote. Unless a person was a registered Republican, it was

very hard for him to land a hotel job or a restaurant kitch-
en job or a license to operate a rolling chair.

There were so many Negroes who lived in Atlantic
City the whole year around that they were, by far, the
majority of voters. Because they had jobs, they owned
houses, thousands of them on the north side of town between the Absecon Bay and Atlantic Avenue. During the
month before elections, the block captains reminded people repeatedly to show up on election day. When the day
arrived, they'd knock on your door at suppertime if you
hadn't yet been to the polling place. You wanted to vote
in any case, to stay on the right side of Nucky's machine.
It was a good deal for everybody.

Charles told me about Nucky's personal touch. If a
hotel maid got sick, a grocery order or a bin of coal could
be expected to be delivered, "With the compliments of
Mr. Enoch Johnson." The Czar might even have stopped
by the lady's house on the North side and left an envelope of spending money until she got back on her feet.
The Republican party – Nucky – donated to the building
committees of the churches. Nucky showed up at Negro
weddings and funerals. He insisted that every block captain and ward leader on the North side call him by his
first name.

That was what Charles Henderson taught me as we
discussed the new President, what a penny bought you in
1929, our children, the weather and what radio shows we
listened to. If you were a Republican politician in the Re-

publican state of New Jersey, you invariably won if Nucky wanted you to win. If he didn't want you to win, you couldn't even get on the ballot. I didn't know it as a matter of fact, but I suspected that Nucky would probably like you a lot if you were to offer him a cash contribution to an Atlantic City charity of his choosing. That was why Nucky was called the Czar, why a United States Senator like Wally Edge had considered it a favor when Mr. Johnson had been kind enough to say hello to, "My good friend in the Justice Department, Edgar Hoover.

The Boardwalk was crowded. There were lots of people waiting in little lines to spend their money. I understood that Charles wanted me to save his job, but I didn't think I had any influence. I changed the subject.

"So," I said, "What about your brother-in-law? Has he been with Hoover a long time?"

"Pierre, he been working for Mr. Hoover for about a year now," Charles said.

"What does Pierre do for him?"

"He take care of the man's clothes, he drive his car, he tell the cleaning girls what to do."

"He's from Washington, your brother-in-law?"

"That's right. Him and Iris and they brothers and sisters, they all from Washington. But Pierre, he got the best job."

"How did he get such a good job?"

"I think they hook up, him and Mr. Hoover, at *Pimlico*."

198

"*Pimlico?*"

"*Pimlico* is the race track in Baltimore. Pierre work there for a long time. He used to be a jockey, back in the day. Pierre, he know all the grooms and the stable boys and the hot riders. He a racing expert. So now, when Pierre drive Mr. Hoover to the track, he go down to talk with the hands about the races. Then he come back up to the grandstand and tell The Man what horses to bet on. They goes to *Pimlico* a lot...Watch the chair!"

It took five minutes to get to the pier by rolling chair. When I stepped onto the boards in the shadowless, incandescent glare of the marquee's myriad bulbs, I said to Charles, "I will see what I can do."

"Thank you, Mr. Albert. I meant no harm at all."

"I understand, Mr. Henderson. But you know I have nothing to do with any hiring or firing." I reached out to shake his hand.

"Just whatever you can do," he said, and took my offered hand.

"Whatever I can do."

A bald man and his wife, seeing the empty chair, immediately asked if it was available. Without waiting for an answer, they stepped onto the footrest and swung their fannies onto the cushion. "How much," said the bald man.

Charles replied. "Five cents a block or a-dollar-fifty a hour."

"Let's do five blocks."

199

"Uptown or downtown?"

Later is When it Hurts

I walked around a queue of people who were in line to see the "*Treasures of the Pharaohs*" exhibition. Seamus, holding himself like a man with a painful shoulder, had returned to his job.

"Good to see you back, Seamus," I said, showing my pass. "How are you doing?"

"Fuckin' awful," he said.

I went up the midway, weaving through the horde of potential photography subjects, delighting in the carnival atmosphere. Decoration Day weekend was shaping up to be, as expected, a bonanza. When I arrived in front of *Memories*, I paused for a few minutes to watch and see how my family was managing. I had no idea that, as I was watching them, I was being watched myself. I probably would have spotted him, had I been looking.

Ida, wearing trousers, was operating the camera and posing the subjects. When she had first taken to wearing trousers in the studio on Chester Avenue, I had been worried, because I didn't know how the customers would react to a lady in pants. When she'd seen the fashion photographs with women in trousers in the Sunday paper, she'd said, "It's about time." I couldn't have talked her out of it if I'd wanted to. None of the customers ever said a word.

She was posing a family of five. The little one sat on the pony statue from the carousel. Ida was saying, "Sit real still on that pretty horsey, now. Is that a nice horsey? Still, now." The kid grinned. Ida snapped the shot, yanked the film holder out and pushed a new one in. She swiveled the camera on its tripod and pointed it toward the cutouts. She posed one of the sisters as the face in the Miss America scenery. Snap. Yank. Push. The other sister had to stand on a stool to be Miss America. Snap. Yank. Push.

Helen was collecting the money, being very sweet and polite about it, making sure the mailing envelopes were correct, double checking that the film holders had the proper tags on them, and promising that the pictures would arrive safe and sound, or the customers would, absolutely, get their money back.

Pauline was taking down the customers' names and addresses and trying to keep them happy as they waited in line. They liked the way she asked where they were from. It seemed as if every place that they came from was, as far as my daughter was concerned, a wonderful place that she had always wanted to visit. Seeing that my little girl was enjoying honest work gave me satisfaction; perhaps she would turn out okay after all.

"I'm back," I announced as the family of five was leaving.

"Albert! Thank God. My arms are killing me. It's your turn," said my wife.

"That's it? 'It's your turn?' No 'Welcome back, we've missed you?' "

I went through a flimsy doorway into the space that I had planned to use as an office. I saw that Gabriel had been very busy, indeed.

A five-foot high stack of film holders without tags was arranged neatly against the wall. Those were the ones from which Gabriel, working blind in the darkroom, had removed the exposed 4 by 5 film sheets and inserted fresh film. An even higher stack of holders, each with a tag, serial numbers with dangling white customer tags was waiting for Gabriel to develop the film sheets.

I recall realizing, as I looked at those two stacks, that I had made some truly dumb mistakes in planning *Steel Pier Memories*. The heavy film holders took up too much space and, compared to roll film, required an enormous amount of effort. I would make the switch to roll film as soon as I could, I vowed, even though I might sacrifice a bit of sharpness in the printing. I was selling souvenirs, for heaven's sake, not fine art. I'd buy at least two more *Rolleiflexes* so that I could have two on the tripods and another ready to go with a fresh roll of film all of the time.

And why had I thought it was a good idea to process the film on the pier? Right then and there, I decided that I would look for a corner in a local warehouse or a garage to set up a darkroom. Then I'd have space for more scenery and for nice chairs for customers to wait their turns in comfort. I hadn't told Hermann how well his ideas had worked out. Did he want to branch out to Atlantic City? He'd be a good partner.

By ten o'clock at night, we were all tired — it was time for everybody, except me, to quit. I gave Gabriel ten dollars, enough to cover his hourly wage, the cost of the room, his train fare, and a little extra for coming down on such short notice.

"You did real good, *boychik*," I told him. "You should sleep late tomorrow. Go to the beach. Take a stroll on the boards. We won't need you until afternoon, about two o'clock." He thanked me and disappeared into the crowd on the midway. I didn't watch him leave. Had I done so, I might have spotted my attacker.

Ida had been pretending, for the girls' sake, that she had not been worried about me and my secrets. The two of us had been smiling all the while, pretending that there was nothing unusual going on, that my sudden disappearances were just normal business. The girls were pretending that they didn't know that we were pretending.

"Albert, enough! Come home with us."

I wanted some time alone — I had a lot to think about. "I won't be long. Just an hour or so. I promise."

After they left, as I straightened things up in the darkroom, I tried to clear the fog of fatigue so that I could focus on my next move.

I thought about Talbot's morning visit, his fury and his threats. Everything would have been finished if I had simply told Talbot that there were no pictures. But I hadn't, and the game was still being played. Why had I not simply told the truth?

I was exhausted, unhinged. Alone, in my tiny work-space, I laughed aloud. I remember thinking that I had become 'a player.' Until that time in my life I had been a worker. Until then, in my mind, there had been a balance between the effort I put into a job and the rewards that the job returned to me. That had been working fine; I had been making a comfortable living and I had been sleeping like a baby. My little universe had been in balance.

Over the weeks leading to Decoration Day, I had learned that men like Nucky, Hoover and Sam *win* power and profits that are enormously disproportionate to their efforts. They didn't work – they *played* at elaborate games where the teams were always realigning, where the rules were weak and constantly being revised. The balance between work and reward was for the average guy, the *schlemozzles* like Al Rubin, not for them. For such players, there is no standard arrangement of cards, no fair deal. If they can't stack the deck, they don't play.

For Hoover, the game had reached an important mo-ment – he was in danger of losing his advantage. If his reputation were to be damaged, he could no longer be sure of winning every hand.

What made me smile as I swept the floor was a deluded sense that I had a feel for the game. As I said, I was exhausted, not thinking straight. I remember congratulating myself on how clever I had been during Talbot's morning visit. Even though I had not planned to deceive him, when he had given me an opportunity to take advantage of him, I had seized it instinctively. Did I have a talent for the sport, or what? Was I truly a player, or what? I was enjoying the game. Besides, it seemed, in my delusional state, that I had a patriotic duty to beat Hoover and Talbot.

Hoover's arrogance and his holier-than-thou attitude *did* bother me – truly, I did not like the G-men. But the real reason I wanted to win, I told my delusional self, was that I was an American doing a patriotic duty. Nucky had it right, even the reincarnation of George Washington should not be allowed to have the kind of power that Hoover held. Wasn't it my job as a real American to best them, to help put limits on their growing power?

I turned out the lights and stepped onto the midway to pull the security gate across the front of *Memories*. Talbot surprised me from behind as I was closing the padlock. He used his forearm on the back of my neck to push my face against the steel lattice. With his other hand, he jammed something small and hard into my back, pinning me.

"When this gun goes off, it will make a teensy little pop, just like the shooting gallery. Nobody will notice. Shall I pull the trigger?" he hissed in my ear.

I was not tired anymore − time slows.

"Shall I?" he repeated, pinning me harder for emphasis. "Later, maybe. Now you're going to come with me. Put your hands behind you."

I had no choice. He snapped handcuffs around my wrists and pulled me around to face him. He had his suit jacket draped over his forearm, covering his hand. He folded the fabric back momentarily so that I could see a black automatic pistol.

"I swear that I will shoot you dead if you do anything I don't like. I will be right behind you the whole way. Do you understand?" He spoke through tightened lips, separating his words, spitting chunks of threat into my face.

He pushed me in the chest, slamming my back into the gate, causing it to clatter loudly, attracting the attention of people on the midway. They stopped and looked toward us.

"This man is under arrest," Talbot announced. "There's nothing to worry about. Keep moving. It's all over."

We covered the distance from *Memories* down to the entrance of the pier and then along the Boardwalk to the *Dennis Hotel* in about fifteen minutes. At night, with the bulbs reflecting off the water, the *Chesterfield* sign was dazzling, with all the different-colored bulbs shining and reflecting off the water. Atlantic City was the most electrified place you could imagine in those days.

He shoved me in the back repeatedly along the way to make sure that I moved quickly. Every now and then someone seemed to notice two grim-faced men in a hurry, one with his hands behind his back. I didn't bother asking for help; he'd have said I was under arrest and waved his Justice Department credentials.

The *Dennis* and the *Marlborough-Blenheim* were the two fanciest hotels in Atlantic City. The *Marlborough-Blenheim* kept Jewish people out by advertising itself as an exclusively "white family hotel" that never had vacancies for Jews. We passed the *Marlborough-Blenheim*, where Hoover and Talbot were staying, and went a block further to the *Dennis*, passing the famous *Traymore Hotel*, which I'd always admired for its fancy Moorish arches and its tiled domes on the roof line. The *Dennis*, I had been told, made Jews feel unwelcome with sneers and terrible service.

The entrance to the *Dennis* was set a half-block back from The Boardwalk, behind lawns and a formal garden. In the middle of the garden, water splashed from tiers down to the round pool of an Italianate fountain. In typical Atlantic City style, to provide a show for strollers on The Boardwalk, a ring of colored spotlights on automatic switches had been set into the flower beds around the fountain. Talbot held me there as the water was turning from green to blue. "Do not look at the doorman. Walk straight to the elevators," he spat. "Do not talk to anyone. Do not give me any trouble." We hurried through the opened door and across the lobby to a waiting elevator.

I got a glimpse of dark furniture, tall potted palms, and oriental carpets. The elevator operator paid no attention to where my hands were; he'd probably seen stranger things.

We got off on the third floor and walked to Room 305. Talbot unlocked the door and pushed me with enough force that I had to stumble through the doorway into a darkened room to keep from falling on my face. He followed after me, locked the door, and switched on a ceiling light that revealed an ordinary hotel room. The drapes were closed.

He turned on the bathroom light and, pointing the gun with one hand, dragged the desk chair into the white tiled bathroom. He pushed me into the bathroom where I stood, hand cuffed, next to the chair, facing him.

He slipped the gun into a shoulder holster. "Where are the pictures?" His open-handed slap to my cheek had the force of a punch.

"Where are the negatives?" Smack.

"Where are they?" Smack.

"You will tell me," he said. Smack. And so on, many times.

When it became clear to him that I would not respond to slaps, he removed the gun from the holster. The weapon filled my vision, the biggest object in the universe.

Instead of putting his finger on the trigger, he positioned it flat in his palm, raised it over his head, and brought the hard steel down onto the bridge of my nose with all his might. I staggered backward and fell over the chair, onto my side on the cold, white floor. Squatting in front of me, his finger on the trigger now, he pointed the gun at my face. "Stand up. Turn around. When I say so, sit in the chair. Understand?"

He intended to undo the cuffs so that he could lace them through the back of the chair. It was probably my last chance; he couldn't keep control of the gun and undo the cuffs at the same time. I faked a rubber-legged weakness, as if the blow to my nose had almost knocked me out and made me helpless. The moment I felt the steel ring loosen from my right wrist, I pushed backward with all the strength in my legs, hoping to catch him off balance.

Still on my feet, I pivoted quickly enough to see him hit the floor. I fell, knees first, onto his stomach. I yanked his head up by the ears, let go, and jabbed the heel of my hand to his forehead. His skull hit the tile with a loud crack, knocking him out.

He was breathing. I put my ear to his chest and heard a rapid, strong heartbeat.

The phone rang in the bedroom. I ignored it.

I found the handcuff key and the gun under the claw foot tub. After I transferred the cuffs from my left wrist to both of his, I dropped the gun into the toilet tank. I set the chair upright. The phone rang as I was dragging Talbot's heavy, dead weight onto the chair; the man was at least six-feet-two and by no means a lightweight. When he was seated, slumped forward, I looked at his face and judged that it was safe to free him for a moment and do what he had intended for me; cuff his hands behind him to the back of the chair.

In the hotel bedroom, the phone had stopped ringing. I unplugged a floor lamp that stood behind an easy chair and used my pocket knife to cut through it. The eight feet of electrical cord was more than enough to tie his ankles to the front legs of the chair.

Boxers don't feel pain in the ring. You can watch a fight and think that a guy who's all bloodied and stagger-ing is hurting. It's not so. When you're in danger, when you're in a fight, you don't feel the blows. Later is when it hurts. Later is when you do the mind tricks to make the pain melt away. I tasted my blood as I breathed through my mouth. My nose felt broken – it was not the first time.

What I saw in the bathroom mirror was bloody mess. The left side of my face was red, purpling, and swollen from his repeated right-handed slaps, the eye almost closed. My nose was flattened, enlarged and askew. I spat blood and looked inside my mouth. I saw that it was cut inside the cheek, but that I still had all my teeth. With a hotel face cloth and hot tap water, I washed the blood off my face, neck, and ears. My collar, shirt, and tie were ruined. I turned off the tap and looked around. Talbot was actually snoring.

Suddenly, I hated the sight of white, octagonal tile, the same kind we had in our bathroom on Chester Avenue. Ida wanted me to put in a built-in shower. We'd go with a real color, I decided.

Someone knocked on the hotel room door as I was stepping out of the bathroom.

Hoover's Gambles

Through the peep hole, I saw Pierre standing on the other side of the door to Room 305. As quietly as I could, I twisted the little handle that unlatched the door. With my back to the wall where the door was hinged, using my hand to muffle and disguise my voice, I called out, "It's open."

I watched the handle turn and the door swing into the room. As soon as Pierre was inside, clear of the door, I slammed it shut behind him and put my back to it.

He took a step backward, toward the bathroom. A switchblade knife appeared in his hand, snapping open with a loud, metallic click. He waved it in front of him in a way that suggested that he was no stranger to a knife fight.

"Where's Mr. Clement," he said.

"Sleeping."

"Who are you?"

"I am a friend of your brother-in-law, Charles Henderson. I am Albert Rubin, the photographer.

"What happened to your face?"

"Talbot hit it with a gun."

"He is sleeping?"

"Yes. In the bathroom. Have a look." I walked deliberately across to the bathroom door and opened it. Talbot was as I had left him.

Pierre, careful not to give me an opportunity to take the knife, looked back and forth from me to the man slumped unconscious in the chair.

"Why is he tied up like that?"

"So he can do me no harm."

"I'm leaving now," said Pierre.

"Please don't."

He tossed the knife into his left hand, then back again, never taking his eyes from mine.

"Pierre," I said, "Charles has asked for my help to keep his job. I'd like to do that. You and I are both responsible for getting him in trouble with the hotel where he works. Please, stay and talk to me, as a favor to Charles, as a favor to your sister, as a favor to me. Truly, I am his friend."

I closed the bathroom door and walked slowly across to the bed and sat on the edge of the mattress. I gestured toward the easy chair. "Please," I said. "Have a seat."

Warily, he went to the corridor door and opened it. I remained perched on the edge of the bed. Apparently satisfied that I did not intend to keep him in the room by force, he went into the bathroom and checked Talbot's pulse. He knelt to look at the G-man's face, rose, returned to the bedroom, closing the bathroom door behind him.

He was a small, trimly built man, very well dressed in a tightly buttoned tan suit and a straw boater hat. He was about my age, perhaps a bit older, with a complexion like caramel. He had large eyes with long, thick lashes.

"I am Albert Rubin," I said, rising and extending my hand. "I am very pleased to make your acquaintance."

He regarded my offered hand skeptically. "I am Pierre Boudreaux," he said. He needed both hands to close the knife. He did so and dropped it into his trousers pocket. Looking warily into each other's eyes, we shook hands. I returned to my perch on the bed and gestured, again, to the easy chair. He removed his hat and hung it on the hook on the back of the door. Mimicking my posture, he sat on the edge of the upholstered chair cushion.

"Why are you here?" I asked.

"My boss couldn't reach Mr. Clement by telephone. I was sent to see why."

I said, "If you don't mind, I would like to be well away from here when you release him."

He did not reply.

"Charles is a good man," I said. Trying to break the ice, I offered him a cigarette. He refused and removed a packet of *Lucky Strikes* from his shirt pocket. I positioned an ash tray between us on the floor. "I have promised to talk to the hotel management about his winter job."

"That would be appreciated," he said, dropping his match into the ashtray.

215

"Did Mr. Hoover tell you what was happening in this room? That Talbot was trying to beat information out of me?"

He shook his head. "Nope. I was surprised to even be let into the room. I was hoping to see Mr. Clement at the door and be told to go away."

"Do you mind if I ask you about your job?"

"You can ask. I probably won't answer," he said.

"I understand," I said, but pressed on. "Charles tells me that you met Hoover at the races. That you are something of an expert."

"Some would think so. I have been a horseman my whole life. I was a jockey, back in the day."

When I first came to this country, in 1903, I studied the sports pages to learn English, to learn about America, and because I like sports. In those days, I'd often see photographs of Negro jockeys. Now, there are only white jockeys.

"That's right, now that you mention it, there aren't any Negro jockeys anymore. How come?"

Dispassionately, as if recalling nothing more important than a bad meal, he said, "They decided they wanted the purses, the white boys did. The track operators and the horse trainers and the owners, they all wanted us out. The white jockeys got into the habit of fouling us in every race, trying to knock us off our mounts, interfering with our horses, and the stewards let them. And then they wanted segregated White-Only and Negro-Only changing rooms. Most tracks never bothered to build Ne-gro-Only ones, and those that did made them from tar-paper and baling wire with no showers, no indoor plumbing of any kind. And then the owners stopped giv-ing us rides, favoring inexperienced white boys whenever they could. Everything just changed, in just a couple of years, back in the aughts."

"I am sorry," I said.

"A lot of fellows got on the boats and went to Europe. I considered it myself. It's funny. American Negroes are taking down nice, big purses at tracks in France and whatnot, but here you can consider yourself fortunate to get a job as an exercise boy." He stubbed his cigarette out. "Not that I'm complaining."

I shook my head, trying to convey my understanding. Jewish people had been living with the same kinds of things for a long, long time. Even in America, although it wasn't as bad as it is in Europe, white Christians make it hard for Jewish people.

If you had been a visitor to Atlantic City, you would have thought that Negroes didn't enjoy the beach or The Boardwalk, because you would never see them there. You would have taken it for granted that Atlantic City was a place for white people only. If you did happen to see a Negro who wasn't working, you would have won-dered how many minutes it would take before a police-man or a lifeguard would show up to make him leave.

217

If you had been a visitor to one of the other shore towns, Wildwood or Ocean City or Cape May, it was the same. There was a difference, though. In towns other than Atlantic City, you wouldn't see any Jewish people on the beaches or on the Boardwalks, either. Atlantic City was the only South Jersey shore town where Jews were permitted, if not exactly welcomed. If you were not a white Christian, you had to watch your step wherever you went.

I said, "So it's a good thing that you were able to get a job with Mr. Hoover. Mr. Henderson believes that Mr. Hoover likes to gamble on horse races. Is that true?"

"Yes, it is."

"I am surprised," I said. "To tell you the truth, I am only slightly acquainted with Mr. Hoover, but he does not strike me as a gambling man."

"He loves it. It is his passion, outside of work. His only passion."

"And he keeps you around to give him inside information?"

"Not *just* that. I am useful to him in many ways. But my connections at *Pimlico* make me more valuable than the ordinary serving man. When I drive him and Mr. Clement to *Pimlico*, I go to the barn to hear what I can. If I've heard something, I tell them. When they win, I get a bit of cash. I've done pretty well for us over the past year."

"What kinds of things do you hear?"

"How a horse has been running on the practice track. If a jockey is sick. That kind of thing. Sometimes it's just a rumor."

"And if he loses?"

"He hates it. Even if it's only a small bet, he gets really upset. He's the kind of person who believes a race has been fixed every time a longshot wins. Most of the time he's mad because he can't find out who to talk to, who has the real inside information. If he thinks I've given him reliable information, unless it is a Communist horse, he sends Mr. Clement to the pari-mutuel window to place a big bet."

Talbot distracted us at that moment. He called weakly from behind the closed bathroom door, "Hello! Hello! Oh, Jesus. Is anybody out there?"

I stood up. "I guess it's time for me to leave."

Pierre rose and stood still, looking toward the closed bathroom door, listening to the frantic cries from within.

"Rubin! Albert Rubin! Are you there? Oh, Jesus!" wailed Talbot. We heard the chair thump against the floor as he tried to kick his legs free.

Quietly, Pierre said, "I will wait a few minutes before I untie him, so you can get clear."

I reached into my pocket and showed him the key to the handcuffs. "You'll need this," I said.

He looked down at the key, then back to my face, wincing in sympathy. "Perhaps not," he says.

I returned the key to my pocket. "Thanks for the information."

He said, "We never met."

"Right," I replied on my way out.

Just before the operator pulled the gate open, I hid the handcuff key in the sand of the ashtray by the elevator. "Going down, sir?"

§

It was after midnight. If Ida had seen my broken nose just then, she would have gone crazy. I decided that I'd best deal with her from a safe distance. I found a phone booth on Pacific Avenue. She picked it up after the first ring.

"Thank God, Al. What's the matter? Why aren't you home? Why didn't you call?"

I reassured her that everything was okay. Then I told her that I wouldn't make it home for awhile —she should go to bed without me.

"I can tell that something bad has happened," she demanded. "Your voice sounds funny. Are you catching a cold? Tell me what happened."

"That fellow Talbot, who came by this morning, he showed up again. We got into a fist fight. I won."

"*Vay is mir*, Al! He is huge. And he works for the Government. This has got to stop! Why can't you come home?"

I said, "I'm okay, don't worry. I'm heading over to *Babette's* to talk to Sam. You're absolutely right, my sweet; it's time to put an end to this *mishugoss*. It's gotten too dangerous."

"So I will see you at the pier?" She said, without enthusiasm.

"No. Let's not open up *Memories*. You must be exhausted. The girls could use a day on the beach. It's Saturday, after all. In fact, let's take the rest of the weekend off. Make sure you let Gabriel know."

"You're sure?" she said happily. "Decoration Day weekend? You're willing to miss all that business? After all our hard work to get ready?"

"We have the whole summer ahead of us."

"Sounds good to me," she answered.

"I'll try to be home before daybreak."

"Don't wake me, you bum."

Telegram

When I walked into the casino, Sam was at the bar on the far side of the room; Mike was behind a group of people playing blackjack. The condition of my face set them both in my direction as soon as they saw me come in. I walked toward the hidden door next to the one-way mirror.

"Mother of God, what happened to your face?" Mike said.

"Let's talk in the office," I replied.

Inside the mirrored room from which Mike and Sam observed the gamblers, Mike switched on a low wattage desk lamp. I wanted to make sure that they knew I was okay, but it hurt my face to smile. I told them the story of Talbot's attack, leaving out my conversation with Pierre. They were outraged, which was fine, it showed me that they cared. But I was not looking for sympathy.

"That son of a bitch. He's not going to get away with this," said Sam.

"Yes he is," I answered. "We don't have to pay him back. Believe me, Clement Talbot is very unhappy right now — he has a terrible headache." Then, I bent the truth a little to keep my word to Pierre. "The housekeepers will find him in the morning, so he's going to have an awful night. When they finally get the handcuffs off him, he's going to have to explain to Hoover that a skinny, unarmed guy got the best of him. That's sorry enough for me."

They protested.

"Listen to me. This is not about revenge. We are in a situation now that's bad for everybody, not just me. The way they came after me shows how serious this is. It has to end."

"How?" asked Mike.

"I have some ideas. First of all, we need Nucky. Will he be here tonight?"

"Every night," said Sam. "He shows up every night. He may be here already."

Mike said, "I'll go see."

When we were alone, Sam looked at me and shook his head regretfully. "Al, I am so sorry. I never expected this to turn out this way. You were not supposed to get hurt. Ida will never forgive me."

That made me want to laugh. Ouch! I'd try to remember not to do any more laughing until my nose got better. "She will get over it. Besides, whenever anything goes wrong, she blames me and nobody else. That's the way our marriage works."

"Well, I'm sorry."

"Good. I am pleased that you are sorry. Now, tell me, if you don't mind, how good are you at fixing horse races?"

His eyes widened and he sat back in his chair. "Personally, I never fix anything. Sometimes, maybe, I know about a fix."

"How about tomorrow? I mean today, Saturday? Can you tell me a winner? Preferably a long shot?"

"You want me to get a race fixed today?"

"The sooner the better. If you can, today would be terrific."

Through the mirrored glass, I saw Mike, Nucky and Louie come into the casino. Nucky could not help but pause and shake a few hands on his way to the office. Inside, after he saw me, Nucky asked, "Are you going to be okay?"

"I'm fine. Actually, the nose has been busted before."

There were not enough chairs for everyone. Louie leaned against the wall and said, "It hurts, no? You look like raccoon! But not cute." His mouth twisted under his handlebar mustache as he laughed at his joke. I guess I did look funny.

When I was sure they were all paying attention, I said, "I have an idea about how we can finish this business as winners. Nucky, guess who was waiting for me with his rolling chair when I left your place this afternoon?" I told them about my conversation with Charles and how worried he was about keeping his job.

"Louie, did you fire him?" I asked.

"Nah. Not yet. Just hollered. A lot."

"He really did nothing wrong. I would appreciate it if you could reassure him that he will have a job next winter."

"What's it to you?" Louie asked.

"We became friends. I'd appreciate it."

Nucky said, "Absolutely. Consider it done. Louie will take care of it." Louie sighed and nodded in assent.

Satisfied that I'd kept my promise to Charles, I told them about Hoover, *Pimlico*, the man's constant quest for inside information, a need so strong that the G-man had hired a horseman with connections as his man servant, and my idea.

Sam argued, "You want to tell the Director of the Investigations Bureau of the United States Department of Justice about a fixed horse race? Are you crazy? *Du bis meshugah?*"

Nucky didn't like it, either. "It goes against my grain to do the bastard any favors. The man is a menace. He should be thrown out of Government service. I can take care of him my way. Wally Edge and I have talked it over. We can put the screws to him in Washington. There are ways."

I let Sam and Nucky rant until they ran out of steam.

"Please, my friends, you need to turn this around. If you continue fighting with him, it will only make him fight back harder. In the long run, you know he will beat you. With all due respect, Nucky, I ask you, what can even a Senator do against J. Edgar Hoover, a man who is a *permanent* Director of a huge bureau with a big, guaranteed budget? A man who might well have a file of secrets on half the Senators in Washington, including Wally Edge?"

I turned to Sam, "What did A. R. say about dealing with politicians? Why can't we treat Hoover the same way A.R. treated the judges in New York? "

"We can't very well make deals with a man who stays away as if we're poison," said Nucky. "If we could talk to him, we could do a little business. Maybe. But that's the problem, he acts like he's as pure as the driven snow."

"He has to talk to us," I said. "He thinks we have the pictures. And, come on, *we* know he's not so pure."

They looked at each other. Sam shrugged, "I'm listening."

Nucky folded his arms across his chest, "Let's hear it," he said.

§

We finished the meeting with a call to *Western Union*. Nucky dictated, "To Mr. J. Edgar Hoover, Guest, Marlborough Blenheim Hotel, Atlantic City, New Jersey. Mr.

227

Hoover-*stop*- Join me for luncheon Sunday noon at Babette's Bath and Turf Club on Mississippi Avenue-*stop*- Disposition of photographs to be decided-*stop*- Jasper Jewel in the second race at Hialeah today-*stop*- Signed Enoch Johnson."

"I need someone with me at the table," said Nucky. "Al, I think it has to be you."

That took me by surprise. "How about Sam? Or Mike? Shouldn't one of you guys be there?" I suggested.

"Too right!" scoffed Mike. "Let the man without a passport or a visa, the man that the Bureau have been asking about on account of certain smuggling and immigration activities, let's let him have lunch with J. Edgar Hoover. It's a lovely idea."

"I feel the same way as Mike," said Sam. "You're out of your mind."

"Louie, you'll be there?" I asked.

"Always," he answered.

Nucky explained, "One never goes to a negotiation alone; it's very bad form. Louie does not negotiate, he intimidates. So, it's you, Albert. And you will be useful. As the photographer, you provide credibility to our curious tale about the pictures. Also, I want him looking at your face; maybe he has some conscience. Furthermore, this is your idea. Confess that you'd like to be present to see how it all turns out."

"Okay," I said. "Maybe I'll finally try a lobster."

Nucky's Offer

I'd seen *Babette's* with the eyes of a man who had wanted to be seduced, through a distorted lens of romance and ambition. Kaleidoscopic images of cut crystal, white linen, polished silver, amber scotch, shimmering gowns and silk dinner jackets had been tumbling in my memory since the night I had first seen the place. On the morning of our luncheon with Hoover, by sunlight, it was just a restaurant.

I was surprised that Babette was there. "Honey, don't I know it!" she said. "This is barbaric, working on a Sunday morning. Sam asked for a private room for a special lunch with all the trimmings. So, for Sam, I am here. You are the first one. Come on back."

"If you don't mind, Babette, can I wait for everybody else in the bar? Have some coffee? Read the newspaper? I've got more than an hour to kill."

I was reminded of Babette's talent for making a man feel important. She ignored the deep purple circles around my eyes and the swelling that barely resembled my nose. She gushed, "Of course. That's a terrific idea," as if my request was as impressive as a scientific discovery. "I'll have Walter bring you a pot of coffee. Will that be all right?" Not only was I great scientist, but a beautiful woman felt privileged to assist me in my noble efforts. What a sucker I can be!

I went into the empty saloon and perched on a leatherette stool. With the Sports section spread across the polished teak of the bar, I found the race results listed in tiny print on the bottom of the next-to-last page. Even though Sam had called me yesterday afternoon to tell me the result, I wanted to see it in black and white. There it was; Jasper Jewel won the second race at *Hialeah* against twenty-to-one odds.

I barely noticed the waiter who poured me a cup of coffee from a silver pot, setting a gilt-edged pitcher of cream and a bowl of sugar cubes down on the bar before he backed away. Sam owned this glitter, I thought. He had just come into enough money to buy another, perhaps fancier restaurant, and he was not even thirty years old. He was living proof that crime pays.

What truly bothered me, at last, as I read the Sports Page of the *Atlantic City Press*, was that Sam felt no shame. The balance between hard work and reward, the fair scales that decent people understand as the foundation of a just world, was a misguided fantasy to him. I like the Sports Page because champions win their crowns on a level playing field by virtue of their talents and effort. Athletics are a kind of proof that the world is fair. It galled me that Sam Brodsky cheated, that he enjoyed his ill-gotten fortune untainted by guilt. Where was the justice if he could cheat and suffer no punishment, not even the self inflicted punishment of a guilty conscience?

I returned to the front section of the newspaper. There was an item about investigations into vice in Atlantic City. Nucky was named as the "Vice Lord," the man who controlled the gambling, the prostitution, and the bootlegging in the Queen of Resorts. That he was. Vice offends a lot of decent people, but *not* because it is unjust. Vice is like any other business: people pay with money and get a measure of satisfaction in return.

I swiveled on the bar stool to greet Louie and his boss when they came in. Nucky was wearing a three piece, pin-striped business suit with a red carnation pinned to the lapel. By daylight, he looked a bit pasty and pouch-eyed; it was the middle of the night for him.

"You could scare a Cossack!" said Louie to me.

Nucky frowned, "Louie, it's not the time for your insults."

"Sorry, boss," he said.

"Honestly, Al, truly," said the Czar, "You look much better than you did yesterday. Really."

"Honestly, Nucky, truly, I would scare the Cossack's horse."

Nucky took the stool next to mine and we spent half an hour discussing our strategy. We were deep in a dis-

231

cussion of the snares we hoped to set when Babette announced that our guests were waiting for us.

Hoover and Talbot were seated at a table in a small, mirrored dining room lit by a crystal chandelier. A vase of lilacs on a sideboard perfumed the air. Talbot and Hoover, seated at the table, did not rise to greet us. Talbot, who seemed to have recovered from being knocked out with a tiled floor, would not look me in the eye. Hoover glared at Nucky.

Nucky broke the ice. "Does everybody know everybody? Mr. Hoover? Have you met my business associate, Albert Rubin? The photographer?"

Hoover inspected my damaged face but said nothing. He did not mind being rude.

"It's okay, Louie," said Nucky. The muscle man nodded and left the room to take up a position outside the door.

As if she was unaware of the tension in the room, Babette cheerfully rattled off the bill of fare, making everything sound special and delicious. There would be lobster that day, but I decided against it. I had enough to worry about at that table; dismembering a crustacean for the first time in my quasi-kosher life was not the sort of challenge I needed. I asked for the club sandwich.

On her way out, Babette said, "I know you gentlemen want your privacy. We'll be sure to knock every time."

When the four of us were alone, Nucky said, "I hope you like the lobster, Edgar. I have been told that Babette has them shipped here from a fisherman in Maine that she knows personally. He puts them in a tank with an electric pump the moment they come off the boat and ships the whole tank to Atlantic City! I think you'll like it."

Hoover flinched very slightly, just a faint tightening of the muscles around his eyes, when Nucky addressed him as "Edgar." Hoover kept silent, waiting for us to raise the subject of the pictures. After all, we had called the meeting.

Nucky said, "Tell Edgar about your business interests, Al. Tell him about the *Steel Pier*. I know he will be interested."

"I've opened a souvenir photo studio on the *Steel Pier*," I said. "Mr. Whitehead and Mr. Dixon, two of your agents, have visited me there. Did they mention it?"

"Are you *the* photographer?" Hoover growled, showing no expression. He tilted his chin down and looked at me, his brown eyes large and slightly bulging, like a bulldog's.

"Yes," I said. "I was in Room 1202 when you and Mr. Talbot were in Suite 1200."

He grunted, satisfied that I had admitted it. Tight-lipped, he said, "I understand you have some pictures of interest to me. Tell me your terms."

233

"Don't worry about the pictures," I said, as if I was talking about something of no importance at all. "The film has been destroyed. Put your mind at ease."

Hoover raised his chin. "Destroyed, you say."

That was the moment I had been rehearsing in my head since I first came up with the idea. I would tell the truth. The tricky part was to make it sound as if I was lying. "Sure. Absolutely nothing to worry about. " I replied.

"In the bosom of the sea. Al, isn't that so?" prompted Nucky.

I cleared my throat and looked down at the tablecloth. "Yep. I threw the film into the ocean." It was a lie, but only a little one.

Hoover looked at Nucky. "Destroyed, Johnson? Utterly? There are no pictures?"

"Not a one," said Nucky offhandedly.

Hoover leaned back in his chair and stared at me, then at Nucky, trying to read our minds. The waiter knocked.

He wheeled a cart into the room and served us ceremoniously, raising each silver dome with a practiced, white-glove flourish and placing our meals, even my humble club sandwich, in front of us as if the meals were treasure. We watched in silence. When he exited, the only sound in the room was the faint squeak of the cart wheels.

Hoover started to say something, then thought better of it. Eventually, he shrugged and leaned forward to begin his attack on the lobster. I watched him twist off a claw, crack it open and dip the meat into a little bowl of melted butter with a tiny fork. He popped it into his mouth and started to chew. "Were there any prints made?" he asked.

Nucky looked at me.

I spoke carefully, as if I had memorized my line. "No, I did not develop the roll. There are no negatives. There are no prints. There is nothing."

In the ring, you look for that moment when the other guy is off balance. Nucky saw his moment and changed direction. "So how long will you be in town?" he asked.

Talbot, working on his very own lobster, said, "We're leaving this afternoon, right after lunch."

Had they agreed that Hoover would do all the talking? The Director shot his companion a look that I read to mean, "Shut up, Clement."

The vice lord started laying the first snare, "Have you had an opportunity to enjoy a casino since you've been in town, Edgar? Do you enjoy wagering at all?"

"I enjoy a friendly bet. I wager on horse races at legitimate race tracks, just occasionally."

Nucky leaned in, "Wonderful sport. I enjoy it myself. I have many friends in the business. Do you have a favorite track?"

"We take a car to *Pimlico*, in Baltimore, on the occasional race day."

"And did you wager on the *Preakness* this year?"

"Unfortunately. I bet on the favorite, but a 12-to-1 horse won. Very strange. And you follow the sport, Johnson?"

"I do enjoy it, " said Nucky. "I recall the *Preakness* very well. It was Dr. Freeland that won, was it not? Certainly, yes, that horse was a 12-to-1 longshot. I fear quite a few people lost money on that race. As it happened, I'd wagered on the winner, so it was fine for me. I'm sorry you had such bad luck."

Hoover's face tightened, "You knew to bet on the long shot! How interesting. Care to share your reasoning with me? The race wasn't by some strange chance, fixed? Was it?" Sarcasm oozed from his question.

Nucky said, "I have many friends in the racing business. I know owners, trainers, jockeys. Very helpful, let me tell you, to have friends in the business."

Hoover's pace with the lobster slowed.

"Let me give you an example. Let's talk about the one I mentioned in the telegram, the second race at Hialeah. It came to my attention, from one of my friends in the business, that Wilbur Munley would saddle up yesterday for the second race at *Hialeah* for his first outing at that track this season. Do you know about Munley?"

Hoover was focused on Nucky's face. "Never heard of the man," he said.

Nucky put some bait above the snare. "Munley almost always rides the winner and rarely finishes out of the money. He is one of the jockeys who, just by being in the race, changes the odds. Yesterday, I knew he was to be on a horse called Jasper Jewel, a green horse that was brought in from Kentucky, just for the purpose of running in the second race at Hialeah, a ten-furlong stakes race with a purse of thirty-five-thousand dollars.

"A mutual friend, a man I trust who knows Munley well, told me that the horse has been practicing at ten fur-longs every day since the beginning of April. As of Fri-day, his times were just a few ticks slower than Man O' War's record for the distance on a dry track. The form, at race time yesterday afternoon, had Jasper Jewel at twen-ty-to-one. I like these odds for this horse for this race, especially with the almost unbeatable Mr. Munley on top. The key for me, along with knowledge that the horse had been specifically prepared for this race, was that it was not to be announced that Munley was to ride until the last possible, legal moment."

Nucky leaned back and asked Hoover, "Do you catch my drift?"

Hoover, without batting an eye, said, "Absolutely. An unknown horse, trained and fast at ten furlongs, is enter-ing a race under a top jockey. The odds are long because

237

the horse's speeds and the rider's identity are unknown until the horses enter the paddock."

"Exactly so," said Nucky. "So, unless I found out that the track was going to be slow yesterday, I would place a wager on Jasper Jewel. In any event, my information did prove reliable and the horse won by a neck. The race was not in any way fixed."

Hoover, ignoring the remains of the lobster, was focused on Nucky. "This friend, why did he give you this information?" he asked.

Nucky nodded. "As I said, I have friends in the racing business for whom I have done favors. At one point, I loaned this fellow, this very astute friend of mine and Munley's, a bit of cash on very favorable terms because he was in a tight spot. It was the least I could do for a friend. So now, to return the favor, if he knows something that I might be interested in, he sends me a telegram suggesting that I might call him. I have done very well with his advice. Certainly, overall, I'm a winner."

Hoover said, "Interesting."

"Is it not?" said Nucky.

Sam told us the same thing, only it hadn't sounded quite the same. Yesterday, before dawn, as we planned our strategy in the casino office, Sam told us about the second race at *Hialeah*. In Sam's telling, the horse was a carefully prepared ringer, the scheduled jockey had been "given good reasons" to back out of the race at the last

238

minute, Munley was the dirtiest jockey in the business, a guy who had been disqualified for fouling almost as often as he had won, and the two favorite horses would both run out of the money, "maybe" because of stomach aches. The astute friend that Nucky claimed is, in fact, a gangster from Miami who begged Sam to take the *Hiale-ah* tip because he is "dangerously" behind on his interest payments on a loan that Sam had given him.

Hoover said, "You know that I was not surprised at the horse's win; your telegram alerted me to the race. But I do not indulge in off-track betting. It is against the law, as you are surely aware. I only wager, legally, at *Pimli-co*." said Hoover.

"Any particular day of the week?" Nucky asked.

"Saturdays," said Hoover. "I can rarely get away any other day."

Nucky nodded and said, "*Pimlico* is a fine track with a wonderful tradition. Actually, my friend knows many of the people there. Yes, actually, as I recall, he told me that he has a permanent box seat above the finish wire that he rarely uses. I'm sure he'd be happy to let you use it whenever he's not there, which is most of the time. Would you be interested?"

"I can't accept any gifts," said Hoover.

"Of course not. But if the box is empty, you should feel free to use it. Why don't I have him get in touch with you?"

Hoover thought for a moment. "A man named Pierre Boudreaux works for me, and he's familiar with the paddocks at *Pimlico*. Why don't you have your friend leave the location of his box in an envelope at the paddock office? If there's no envelope there, then I'll know that your friend intends to occupy the box on that Saturday."

Nucky took a fountain pen and little notebook from the inner pocket of his suit coat. "Pierre Boudreaux, you say?"

"Yes. A Negro."

"And if my friend has any useful information about a race, perhaps he could put it in the same envelope," said Nucky casually. Hoover did not reply. There was not much left of his lobster. He cracked open the creature's head. I saw some green goo that made me think again about whether I would ever eat one of the things.

Nucky changed direction. "I hope you enjoyed the G.A.R. Ball to inaugurate our Convention Hall. I was so pleased that Wally Edge invited you."

"It was okay," said Hoover. "I don't dance."

"Wally tells me some terrific things about you. He claims that you have, single handedly, created the most efficient bureau in all the federal government."

"That's nice of him," said the Director modestly.

"I know Wally very well; he's a shrewd man who is not easily impressed. Yet he cannot stop talking about you. He tells me that your bureau has gotten increased funding every single year that you have testified."

"I suppose that's true," said Hoover.

"You know it is. But I'll tell you what really impresses Wally, and, I must confess, me too. It's the job you are doing for our country."

"Well," said the Director, "That's very kind of you."

"That you have been able to accomplish so much at your age is downright amazing. You are the Investigation Bureau's first *permanent* director, are you not? That alone is an accomplishment and says that a lot of men in Washington, not just Wally Edge, appreciate your dedication." Flattery *a la* Rothstein was a piece of our strategy.

"Please. Enough."

"All right. Enough is enough. I just want you to know that I admire what you're trying to do and that you have my support from here in New Jersey," Nucky said.

Hoover used the finger bowl and wiped his hands. "Well, I appreciate it. We do better when state and local officials give us their support." This sounded less than whole-hearted. It was the kind of thing Hoover probably said whenever he testified to the committees in Congress.

Nucky pressed on, "Absolutely. Nobody can go it alone. But I do have a certain influence, because I have a kind of unique position that you should feel free to call upon."

"What kind of influence are you referring to?" said Hoover, clearly intrigued.

"I know gangsters. I have to."

"Go on," said Hoover after a pause.

Nucky sighed, "It's no secret that our town offers visitors, especially our conventioneers, opportunities to indulge themselves. Here in Atlantic City, we do not judge. Even if a man chooses to take his pleasures in unusual ways, if there is no harm done, if no one gets hurt, Atlantic City does not judge."

Hoover was studying the bubbles in his glass of water. Talbot was looking at the salt shaker.

"You are a man of the world," Nucky intoned, looking at Hoover. "You know what I mean. Men of stature rightly do not indulge themselves in the towns and cities where they live. There, they abide by good American standards of decency and morality. Rightly so; this is as it should be.

"Here, in Atlantic City, we have two very distinct sets of standards. On the beaches and The Boardwalk, our standards are the same as any American town's, perhaps even stricter because the children and the wives are there. The ladies and the children should not in any way be troubled by any kind of indecency. But, off the Boardwalk, on our back streets, grown men are free to indulge their natural inclinations in places like the *Entertainers Club* and a hundred other establishments. My responsibility is to make sure that those establishments conduct their businesses unobtrusively and discreetly. What happens here is strictly between a man and his companions. It stays here." The way Nucky put it, he was providing a necessary public service, like clean, running water.

Hoover studied the Czar. Talbot picked up the pepper shaker, apparently fascinated by the way the little black and gray flecks rolled around inside it. By referring to *the Entertainers Club*, Nucky had clearly announced that he knew about Hoover's secret preferences.

"So, Edgar, you can begin to see the special nature of my influence. The people who provide these services cannot operate here, I do not permit it, unless they abide by our standards. Nor do I encourage freelancing. By that, I mean that I prefer to exert my influence through their employers, some of whom are known as gangsters in other cities. For example, let me tell you about me and Scarface Al Capone."

Babette knocked and poked her head in to see if we were ready to have the table cleared. The fancy china was loaded onto the cart and wheeled away. Babette personally refilled our water glasses. Nucky said to her, "I'll have Louie come find you when we are ready for dessert."

Nucky continued after she left. "Al Capone and some other men, gangsters every one, held a convention, of sorts, in Atlantic City just a few weeks ago. I will tell you the names of some of the invited conventioneers because

243

it illustrates the point I am making about my special influence with this sort of person. Charles Luciano and Sam Brodsky came from New York. Are you aware of those men?"

Hoover and Talbot exchanged a glance. Hoover said, "Very much so."

"And Max Hoff, Nig Rosen and Waxy Gordon came from Philadelphia?"

"Their names have appeared in reports, yes," said Talbot.

"Do you know of Charles Polizzi, Moe Dalitz and Lou Rothkopf from Cleveland? These men were at the gathering." Nucky recited a long list of names and cities. Hoover and Talbot nodded when they heard a familiar one. Nucky seemed to know an awful lot of gangsters.

He leaned toward Hoover, "For men like this, Atlantic City is like the League of Nations. Do you see? These men are rivals. In some cases, they are mortal enemies. But here, they come without concern for their safety. A goodly number of these people have business interests here. They own property. They have restaurants and other establishments managed by proxies. So, you see, Edgar, these men need my good will. They want to stay on Enoch Johnson's good side."

Hoover said, "What about Capone? You were about to explain that you had influence."

"Yes, I was. During the gathering that I am speaking of, Capone made a public display right on Pacific Avenue, in broad daylight. He took exception with the manners of a desk clerk at his hotel and dragged the poor fellow out into the street. I was present, doing my duty as a welcoming host. It was clear to me that Capone was ready to beat the poor guy, maybe even shoot him. The man is a brute, the kind who sees no virtue in controlling his temper. I, personally, restrained him with the assistance of the doorman and some bellhops. To make a long story short, Al Capone was severely criticized about that incident by myself and all of the other men who'd been invited to the convention. As a result, he made amends with the staff people at the hotel, apologized, and paid a handsome bonus to the clerk."

"That's it?" says Hoover, scornfully. "You made him apologize? That's the kind of influence you have? I am not impressed."

Nucky sipped water from his crystal tumbler. "Of course not. But the point here is that, as a result of those meetings, just two weeks ago, right here in Atlantic City, Al Capone agreed to cooperate with his rivals. These are men who know only the streets. In the past, they've settled scores with fists, knives, bats and guns. You know, you must be aware, as every citizen is aware from reading his newspaper, that the number of killings has been rising steadily, year by year, ever since the end of the

Great War. The St. Valentine's Day Massacre in Chicago this past February got everyone upset. The Department of Justice must be concerned and rightfully so. Well, Edgar, I can tell you that the numbers are now going to go the other way."

Hoover stared at Nucky. "You! You can make this assurance!"

Nucky replied, "Headlines about murder are bad for business. The men who came for our little convention provide the same kinds of services in their cities as do our off-the-Boardwalk establishments here in Atlantic City. The difference is that the double standard, that is so obvious here, is denied in their towns. Here, there is no hypocrisy. In places like Cleveland, Chicago and Philadelphia, it's a different story. There, the minions of the law are compelled to act against anyone who makes the headlines. The ministers and the Temperance League ladies march on the City Halls and the next thing you know, the whole apple cart gets knocked over.

"Notoriety is a bright light that the men who came for our little convention cannot stand. Since the Saint Valentine's Day Massacre, the headlines were getting bigger and the light kept getting brighter. The men from New York, Brodsky and Luciano, organized the convention to try to get the others, particularly Capone, to behave more sensibly, for their own good. I had to be involved, if only

peripherally, because Atlantic City was the logical location for the gathering to take place."

Nucky paused and looked at Hoover. Sounding surprised, he said, "Edgar, did you not know about our little
convention?"

Hoover did not reply.

Shaking his head in wonderment, the Czar said, "So,
you, the Director of the Investigations Bureau of the
United States' Department of Justice, had no knowledge
of the fact that the twenty-five most notorious gangsters
in America were together in one place for a week. Edgar,
not only did I know about it, I was here. And do you
know what else was remarkable about that convention,
Edgar? Those men agreed to cooperate with one another."

Hoover, offended by Nucky's mocking tone, decided
to counter-attack, "A conspiracy!" he said. "With you at
the heart of it! In the name of all that's holy, Johnson,
why are you telling me this? Don't you know what I can
do to you?"

"Please," said Nucky. "I am well aware of the powers
of your office. I thought I had made it clear that I respect
them and that I admire you for having seized them. I am
not a lawyer, Edgar, but I'm sure that you couldn't prosecute based on anything I've just told you. Please, stop
your posturing. You can't take this to court, and you

know it. And you shouldn't want to. You have much bigger fish to fry."

"Who the hell are you to tell me my job? Me? Posturing? You have the most unbelievable nerve of any man I've ever met! I'll prosecute you or anyone else I choose to. I make those decisions and no one else, least of all, the likes of the Treasurer of Atlantic County New Jersey."

Nucky Johnson pushed back from the table. Before he rose, he said, "Edgar, take hold. I'm offering you a gift. There is opportunity for you here. Let's think about it over dessert, why don't we. Do you like cheesecake?" He went to the door and said to Louie, "Tell Babette we're ready for the next course."

"Wait until you see this dessert, tray, Edgar. It's magnificent." Nucky seemed completely oblivious of Hoover's anger.

Clement Talbot was finally willing to look at me. I did not care for his little smile, he seemed amused by the condition of my face.

"Headache? Seeing straight?" I inquired. I gestured at his deeply bruised, scratched and swollen wrists, "Did that to yourself, did you?" He stopped smiling.

Babette led a procession of white-jacketed waiters into the little dining room. One wheeled a cart with a three-tiered, silver dessert tray. A second pushed a bar cart with brandy and liqueurs. The third waiter steered a cart holding a coffeepot and gilt-edged china. The white-gloved head waiter served us.

Nucky said, "Babette carries a Spanish brandy that is magnificent, Edgar. Thirty years old. Truly exceptional. You should give it a try, Edgar."

Hoover sighed and said, "Alright. I suppose there's no harm in it." The waiter poured a copper colored liquid into the bowl of an enormous brandy snifter and placed it ceremoniously in front of The Director. Talbot asked for something called "*Kwon Troe*," which was clear as water.

"Just coffee, for me," I said.

By the time we had been served and the waiters had departed, much of the tension had left the room. Beautiful food and anger, somehow, don't mix. Hoover had turned his attention to the chocolate, the fruit and the whipped cream

Nucky said, "Edgar, what I meant to say, is that I believe that there are much greater threats to the safety of our country than vice. You can't honestly believe that the federal government should waste its resources chasing bootleggers, gamblers and prostitutes of various male and female persuasions when the Communists are trying their best to destroy our way of life. We should leave the enforcement of the vice laws to the locals, don't you agree? That's all I meant."

Hoover did not bat an eye at Nucky's reference to male prostitutes, something I'd never imagined. Instead, he admired the way the brandy coated the snifter, inhaled a noseful and took a sip. He raised his eyebrows in a way that said he liked it. "You're right about the Reds. They are the real threat alright, " he said. "No doubt about it. But I have no choice. Congress has to listen to its constituents. Capone and the others are causing letters to be written and petitions to be issued. Inevitably, when I ask for my budgets, Congress asks me what I'm doing about crime and vice."

"That's exactly my point. Let me help you," said Nucky. "I won't provide evidence, but, as I said before, I have influence. Let me know which Congressmen are complaining loudest and, I promise you, I will exert business pressures on those who are causing the most trouble."

"Business pressures? What do you mean?"

Nucky thought about it for a moment. "For example, Edgar, I know many of the men involved with illegal liquor importation. At my request, they would be willing to selectively raise an individual's prices or delay distribution to that individual if I were to ask them to do so."

Hoover considered that and seemed to accept it.

"There are other ways, too," said Nucky. "I make it my business to know the chiefs of police and the judges who come here for their national conventions. Many men in law enforcement, such as yourself, although not nearly as high-ranking, think of me as a friend and colleague. I roll out a nice, red carpet of hospitality to my friends when they come to town.

"Occasionally, it happens that certain bad customers leave Atlantic City without paying their debts or after having hurt someone. We don't want these people ever to come back. I have often asked high ranking police officers, even chiefs, my friends, to find these bad customers and remind them of my influence.

"You may find this hard to believe, Edgar, but, just like yourself, I am in the law enforcement business. Take my word for it, I am able to have the laws governing the off-Boardwalk businesses enforced in most of our big cities.

"I am offering you my friendship and the benefit of that influence. You can divert the scarce resources of the Investigations Bureau away from tracking down the Communists. You can spend thousands of hours building cases against petty criminals. Or you can give Enoch Johnson a call."

Hoover had finished his plate of desserts. He looked at his wristwatch. "You are too generous," he said sarcastically. "In return? Whatever must I do to earn the benefit of such influence?"

Nucky sighed. "Just call me and let me know who the politicians want investigated. I'll take care of it from there."

"That's all? Just call you?"

"Yep. It will prevent surprises. Nobody likes surprises. In particular, the kind of people who own our off-Boardwalk businesses, would feel indebted to me if I was able to warn them of unpleasant surprises. Everybody wins. The Congressmen will cease to have cause for complaint and will, therefore, cease annoying the Justice Department. The businessmen will be given fair warning in order to avoid trouble with the authorities, and I will have earned their gratitude."

They stared at each other.

Nucky looked away from Hoover and said to me, "Al, no one has to worry about any pictures, am I right?"

I was taken by surprise, thinking that they had finished with that piece of business. "Uh, no," I said. "I guess not."

"Let's do this," said Nucky. He checked the time on a slim watch on a fine gold chain that he lifted from his vest pocket. "I know you have to get back to Washington, and I have a funeral to attend. Why don't you think this over for a week or so. Meanwhile I will get in touch with my friend and see if he's alright about letting you use his box *at Pimlico*. If you call me asking for my help with some troublemaker, that would be excellent. If you don't,

252

then there's no harm done. I leave it entirely up to you."
Nucky stood.

J. Edgar Hoover pushed his chair back, stood up, and said, "Thanks for the lunch."

"My pleasure," said Nucky. "Let me know the next time you plan to come to town, and I'll see to it that you get the kind of red-carpet hospitality a man in your position deserves."

"Don't count on it," said J. Edgar Hoover.

Barefoot on the Beach

T he steel trusses of the jetty's light tower were more substantial than they had seemed from the deck of the *Sweet Emma*. It was a bright Wednesday morning in early August, hours before we would open for business on the pier. Ida and I had stepped from rock to rock, out to the end of the jetty, a spot where we liked to watch waves break against the rocks and listen to crying gulls and hissing foam.

"You know," said Ida, "I am definitely getting used to this. And we have Sam to thank."

"It's not that I don't appreciate what he's done for us. I do. I have told him so. But I absolutely do not want to be in his debt."

"I don't think he feels that you owe him anything," Ida defended.

"Well, I have to be sure. He knows, because I made a point of telling him, that I am ignoring the dollar-a-month rent that it says in the lease. I paid Hamid the August rent at the going rate, just like I did for July, plus a hundred extra for back rent in May and June. By the end of September, we'll be all square."

"Big shot," she said. "Mr. Rolling-in-Dough."

"Do you want Sam asking any more favors from me? One broken nose is enough, thanks." I could finally shave without being appalled by my visage.

"Just kidding, Al. What did Sam say when you told him about the rent."

"He laughed at me. He said I was nuts."

"Did you tell Nucky?"

"No. I haven't seen him or Louie since the lunch with Hoover. We have different hours, you know. Right now, he's just crawling into bed."

"Not alone, I bet."

"Probably with some showgirl. Maybe two or three."

A few men stood fishing on rocks along the ocean side of the jetty. If I ever get some time, I thought, I would like to try my hand at fishing. We watched a cabin cruiser come up the Inlet toward us. It passed the light tower, made a lazy turn to the right, to the west, along the beach. The high rise hotels and the Convention Hall were, I imagined, an impressive sight from the sea. Maybe I'd save up and get a boat.

"So, you don't know what happened with Hoover. Whether he's been calling Nucky or sitting in the box at *Pimlico*."

"Oh, he's using the box. Sam says that Pierre picked up the envelope the very next Saturday and that they've been coming to the track almost every week since."

"Has Sam been putting racing tips in the envelope?"

"I didn't ask. I guess so."

"It's amazing to me that Hoover thinks you have the pictures, even though you told him you didn't," said Ida.

"I gave an excellent imitation of a liar, if I do say so myself. But even without the pictures, he understands that Nucky could destroy him. *He* knows that *we* know he's queer. Rumors, especially if Nucky spreads them to his high-powered Washington friends, would be devastating to a man in Hoover's position. The pictures aren't even necessary."

"It's sad, isn't it," said my good wife.

"It would be sad if Hoover wasn't the kind of man who thinks it's okay to listen in on people's telephone calls, who thinks nothing of arresting people because he doesn't like their politics, who sends people away to foreign countries without evidence. No, I can't muster any sympathy for such a man. Besides, now he can come to Atlantic City and be queer to his heart's content. Nucky just about gave him the keys to the city. So, there's nothing to be sorry for."

"I'm surprised that you and Nucky didn't make a big deal about the telephone office and the lady who's being paid to listen to Nucky's calls."

"Nucky had a friend in the telephone company put in another line with an unlisted number. He'll use that one when he doesn't want Hoover listening in. Sometimes, he might use the regular line just to give Hoover something to think about."

Ida smiled. "And Sam? Is he satisfied?"

"Not satisfied, but definitely less worried. He was glad to hear that Hoover will be chasing Communists first, and only come after criminals like Sam when he has to."

"Do you think Hoover will do what Nucky said? Call him about the gangsters that the politicians want him to go after?"

"Who knows? What Nucky was really saying was that he wants lines of communication between them. I guess when it suits Hoover's purpose, he might give Nucky a call. Time will tell. What Nucky is sure of is that Hoover heard both the threat of a rumor campaign and the promises of good things that come with Nucky's friendship. It's a combination that Hoover, who's nobody's fool, can't really refuse.

"Time to go," I said.

"No hurry," said my wife.

We made our way back to The Boardwalk, stepping carefully from one rock to the next. We leapt off the jetty into the soft sand and walked a few paces to stairs leading to The Boardwalk. Our shoes were where we had left them. We sat on the steps and slapped the dry sand off our feet. The Boardwalk is narrow along the Inlet because there are no rolling chair lanes. There were no shops or game parlors, just a mile-long promenade under which gentle waves lapped softly onto a narrow beach. Five blocks from the jetty, the house on Rhode Island Avenue had become the Rubin home. We walked toward it slowly, savoring the day.

§ **The End** §

ABOUT THE AUTHOR

Stanley Cutler writes historical mystery thrillers set in the mid-Twentieth Century, literary fiction, and essays on politics, communication, and human nature. He draws on the experience of several careers, most recently as a planning consultant for Fortune 500 companies and government agencies. Earlier careers include computer programming, art salesman, real estate manager, and teacher at universities and public schools in the USA and abroad.

His other works include continuations the Rubin family story as the Dave Levitan Mystery Series:

THE HOMEFRONT a Dave Levitan Mystery

KILLER MATH a Dave Levitan Mystery

KNOTS a novel about cultural upheavals in the 1970s

TWO CONVENTIONS essays on political evolution

(see **www.stanculterauthor.com**)